I0541074

Whiskey for Breakfast

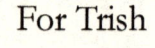
For Trish

Whiskey for Breakfast

A Nick Dioli Mystery

Dominic Stabile

Winter Reading Press - South Carolina

~

Copyright ©2014 Dominic Stabile. All rights reserved.

This is a work of fiction. Names, characters, places and incidents are either the product of the author's imagination or are used fictitiously, and any resemblance to actual persons, living or dead, business establishments, events, or locales is entirely coincidental.

Cover design by SelfPubBookCovers.com/yvonrz and layout by Dominic Stabile.

Published by dominicstabile.com in alliance with Winter Reading Press.

Printed in the United States of America

First Edition: 2014

ISBN: 0692299270
ISBN-13: 978-0692299272

Whiskey for Breakfast

Chapter One

I watched the second floor window of the Cupcake Factory. It was a long shot Chelsea would move to that window, if she was here at all. But it was the only way I was going to see her without her seeing me.

The Cupcake Factory was a small bakery located in downtown Gatlinburg, one of a dozen shops along the Parkway. It had a false front meant to give it the appearance of an old southern home. But from the alley it looked like all the other buildings in town: a cold, concrete block. It was owned and operated by Chelsea's grandmother on her mother's side. A nice old lady. Hair balled up and stuffed into a hair net. Eyes big and watery behind thick lenses. A short, frail old lady. Thin wrists. Harsh smile lines on her red cheeks. A chrome 1911 in her rosy-pink apron with yellow tassels dangling from the front pocket like something you'd expect from an old couch pillow.

I'd gone inside an hour ago to speak to the old lady about her granddaughter, Chelsea. Chelsea's father, a judge named James Tully, was very interested in knowing where she'd run off to. Her mother was dead, the funeral was in two days—it made sense to me her father would want her around.

Grandma had taken one look at me and her hand went down into that pocket. I got halfway through my first question before the 1911 rose up on the end of that hand, an inch-around black eye staring me down from its polished muzzle. The contrasting emotions of fear brought on by the gun aimed at my face and nostalgia triggered by the homey scent of freshly baked cupcakes was disorienting.

I laughed.

She disengaged the safety.

The only other person in the building was a fat man wearing a flannel button down shirt tucked, with great effort, into a pair of brown slacks. He sat at a nearby table, sweat running down his face, mouth moving as he chewed his fourth or fifth cupcake. Crumpled cupcake wrappers littered his table. He watched to see what she was going to do with the gun, his face shiny and expressionless—the face of someone on task with his eating.

"I'm with the police," I said.

"See your badge," she said.

I kept expecting the bell over the door to *ding*. But the morning is not a popular time for cupcakes.

"Think hard before you ask me what you was about to ask me," she said.

I ordered a cupcake and left. I wasn't going to get anywhere that way.

I went around the corner and sat on a bench in front of a shop that sold figurines made of glass. I ate my pumpkin spice cupcake, starting with the toasted marshmallows on top. Then I ate the cake part, and finished off the icing in one bite. I sat there a minute and watched the mountains beyond the I-Hop across the street. The sky was gray. A mist draped the mountains like an unruly nightgown. The air felt like it had rain in its future, and there was a smell of wet cedar. I stayed there a while and just watched like that, something I've begun to do often.

Whiskey for Breakfast

Once I was confident Grandma had some customer traffic to distract her, I'd circled around the block and come up through the alley from the back. And here I was, staring up at this window, waiting for a young woman's shadow to come into view.

Chelsea's father had given me the address to the Cupcake Factory. He said it was the most likely place she would go to get away from him. I'd already checked the old lady's house, just to be sure, and found no sign the girl had even spent the night there. Based on the welcome I'd received from Grandma, I felt good about that room over the shop.

"Did my dad send you?" A voice off to my left.

I nearly lost some skin twisting so quickly in the narrow space. A girl. Maybe thirteen. She wore white-washed jeans, a dark purple jacket. Long blond hair hung down to just below her waist. The skin around her eyes looked raw.

"Chelsea?" I said. Just after I said it, I saw the gun handle in her right hand. She had as much of the gun concealed in her right jacket pocket as would fit.

"Did my dad send you?" she said again. A tremor in her voice. Jaw clenched.

"He's worried about you," I said. I'd raised my hands without being asked to. "He's grieving. He wants you there."

"He wants me dead," she said, and her voice broke on the word "dead."

She pulled the hand from her right pocket and the gun came with it.

My hands went higher. "I don't know anything about that."

"Did you ask him why I ran?" she said.

"Why don't you put the gun away," I said. "Put the gun away and let's talk." I could feel the weight of my own gun against my ribs, just under my left arm, but I wasn't about to draw on a 13-year-old girl.

She raised the gun a little, aimed it in my direction. "Why did he send you?"

9

"I'm a private investigator," I said, finding that I barely had enough oxygen in my lungs to spit out the words. "Your father asked me to find you and bring you home safe."

"Then why did you bring a gun?" she said. Raising my arms had spread open my jacket. She could see the handle of my gun in its holster.

"Sometimes the jobs I take are dangerous."

She stared at me, her eyes wiser than her thirteen years. "Do you ever work for bad people?"

"I don't ask a lot of questions," I said. "So, yeah, probably."

"My dad's a bad person," she said, lowering the gun. "You should have asked questions."

There was movement behind me, a vague scrape of shoe rubber over sandy pavement. But I didn't register the sound at the time. I would remember it when I woke up an hour later.

I was in a bed more comfortable than my own. Cool air on my face, almost like soft fingertips. I opened my eyes. Brown fan blades spinning slowly against a cream ceiling. Chelsea and the fat man who'd downed six or seven cupcakes stood over me, grim, like people paying their respects. The fat man had some icing on his upper lip.

I said, "You have some icing on your upper lip," and my voice sounded like an empty soup can hitting the side of a metal building.

The fat man wiped his upper lip, then inspected the substance on his finger to make sure it was in fact icing. Then he licked it off. "He's 'wake," the man said, looking over his shoulder. He backed up, and the old lady came into view.

It might be that our first encounter had soured my perception of her, but she didn't look like a nice old lady anymore. There was something to the effect of river rocks about her eyes. Hard, dark. How did she ever sell a cupcake a day in her life with eyes like that? She'd lost the apron, and now wore clothes more befitting yard work. Red plaid shirt tucked into blue jeans. A fixed-blade knife with a stag handle hung from her belt by a leather sheath. Her hair was down. Silver strips of it spilled over either shoulder, stopping just above her navel.

"Go get some water," she said, taking those eyes off me just long enough to glance at Chelsea. Chelsea stared at me another moment, then left the room.

My arms felt numb, but I managed to lean up onto my elbows. My brain rolled forward inside my skull, and my vision went blurry.

"Easy," the old lady said. She took a second pillow and slipped it under my head so I could sit up. "Got some questions for you before you pass out or die or whichever happens."

"Virginia?" the fat man said. He was kneeling in front of a fireplace about ten feet from the foot of the bed. He gave her a disapproving look, then turned and stabbed a poker into the glowing coals. She turned to look at me. The eyes had softened some.

"That wasn't very Christian of me," she said. "But neither is trying to kill my granddaughter."

I had my arms back. I could feel my toes pressing against the tightly tucked bed sheets. With effort, I reached up and touched the back of my head. There was a bandage there, held on by gauze that wrapped around and across my forehead. I tried to stretch and found my arms were tied to the headboard with cord. They'd left me just enough slack to pick my nose if I wanted.

"Who tried to kill who, now?" I said. My voice was starting to sound like my voice again, but I worried it betrayed a little of my apprehension.

Her eyes narrowed, and she sat on the edge of the bed. She leaned in closer, and I could smell the morning's baking on her. The fireplace crackled as the fat man added a log. I looked around for the gun she'd had, then guessed she must have left it in her apron.

"If her daddy sent you, it was for one reason," she said. "And it sure as hell wasn't so you could bring her back safe and sound."

Chelsea entered the room with a plastic pitcher and a tall red cup. She filled the cup with water from the pitcher and handed it to me. I hadn't realized how thirsty I was. I downed the first cup quickly, and she poured me another.

"That's the job," I said. I chugged the water, spilling some down my chin and onto my shirt. "He told me to find her and bring her back safe."

"Why did he call *you?*" Virginia said.

"He didn't," I said. "I've got friends around who keep their eyes open for freelance jobs. A friend of mine told me about Tully's predicament. Tully was still deciding what to do when I contacted him, offered my services."

"Why do you think he trusts you with his daughter's safety over the police?" Virginia said.

"I didn't think about it," I said. "A paycheck's a paycheck." And this was true. I hadn't thought about it. I'd taken dozens of missing persons cases where the client, usually someone prominent like a judge, didn't want to make a big deal about the situation, get in the newspaper over it. "Besides," I said. "Tully knows she's here. He just needed someone to bring her home. That's me."

Virginia yanked the now empty cup from my hand. She stood and set the cup on a desk in front of a window facing the alley. The window I'd been watching earlier. She stood there looking out as if she could see anything besides the gray wall of the next building. The light coming through was as gray as that wall. As gray as the mist that had probably left the mountains by now. She pressed her fingertips against the desktop. Leaned there like that. Quiet. And it was then I realized she was debating in her mind whether or not to kill me. I didn't know why, but I knew that rigid posture, that wandering look in the eyes. I knew my hands were bound, and one of these nice people had tried to bash my skull in.

Something had them scared; and frightened people are unpredictable. If Virginia thought I truly was a threat to her granddaughter, she'd do what she had to do to protect her. I could see that burden in the way she leaned there at the window.

The fat man had a good fire going now. The logs hissed and crackled soothingly. He hung the poker on a rack next to the stone hearth, then sat down in a rocking chair. "Come on over here, Chels," he said without turning his head. His rocking chair creaked softly. He kept his eyes on the fire.

Chelsea walked over to him and sat in the rocking chair next to his.

They creaked. The fire crackled. And Virginia stood there thinking in that gray light.

"I feel like we're waiting for something," I said.

She didn't move. "My niece'll be back up in a few minutes. She'll be able to tell me who you really are, and then we'll know what to do next."

"Unless your niece is a mystic, your best bet's to take my word for it. Or check my investigator's license."

"She has your license," Virginia said. "She's downstairs in her cruiser running it now."

"Your niece's a lady cop," I said.

"A detective," Virginia said, turning her head away from the window to glance at me. The light made deep caverns in the wrinkles of her face. "A real one."

"Why are you so sure I'm here to kill Chelsea?" I said, tugging lightly on my restraints, testing them.

She turned away from me quickly, as if to hide something her face might give away. "Stop pulling on your ropes," she said.

"You wouldn't be willing to untie me, would you?"

She turned from the window and sat down on the edge of the bed again. Hands crossed on her lap. I could see the knife from this angle. Judging by the length and shape of the sheath, it was a six-inch Bowie (eleven and one quarter, counting the handle). The stag handle was polished and smooth, but it was not factory made. You could tell by the awkward shape and the irregular pattern of the ridges and color. It was the real thing.

She was looking down at the floor. She seemed to think for a moment, then looked at me. Her expression was patient. Almost apologetic. "I hope you are who you say you are," she said. "If you aren't, I'll have to kill you. I believe God would damn me for it, if I wasn't damned already. But I won't have a choice." She let out a long breath, gripped her knees, and stared down at the floor. Then she crossed her hands on her lap again, took a deep breath, and turned to me. I noticed the color of her eyes for the first time. They were blue. A new moisture made them shine, and removed the stony darkness they'd held earlier. "If you are who you say you are—" She paused, as if to catch her breath. She was struggling to keep her voice firm and even. "If you are who you say you are, I need your help."

Footsteps outside the door. Virginia stood as a woman entered the room. The woman was tall, at least five foot ten. She wore a long brown jacket over black slacks. Her hair was strawberry blond, closer to blond. Black, heeled shoes clanked against the floor boards as she crossed over to where Virginia stood.

"He's legit," she said. She looked at me. "You're awake."

"You're the lady cop," I said.

"Detective," she said, and then she turned back to Virginia. "Just set him loose, Aunt V."

"He can help," Virginia said.

"We can do this ourselves."

"I don't want you involved in this," Virginia said.

"I'm already involved," Lady Cop said. "And I have the resources to keep Chelsea safe." She walked over and sat on the edge of the bed, where Virginia had sat a moment ago. She unlatched the knife from Virginia's belt and held it a moment, blade lain across one hand. It was Damascus steel; a strong, murky metal.

She used the knife to cut my restraints. I sat up, slowly this time. Lady Cop stood by, knife in hand as I stretched and reoriented myself. I pressed lightly on my bandage. It was tender.

Lady Cop handed me my license. "You're free to go," she said.

"No chance I could leave with the kid?"

"None," Lady Cop said.

"I don't suppose you'd change your mind if I threatened to report this to your superiors?"

Lady Cop stared at me. Her eyes were nowhere near as hard as Virginia's. There was an unmistakable tenderness in them, as well as fear. Whatever these people were dealing with, I was thankful they were giving me the door.

"I hate to disappoint the judge," I said, getting to my feet. I found my jacket slung over the headboard. "But if that's the only way you'll have it." I glanced at Virginia. She had a fist pressed against her lips. Her eyes were big and moist.

Lady Cop turned to hand Virginia the knife, and when she did I casually slipped my cell phone from my jacket pocket and placed it on the night stand. I looked Virginia in the eyes as I did this. The fat man and Chelsea were still watching the fire. The fat man was whispering something to Chelsea.

"I'd better get going," I said, and left.

Downstairs, the bakery was empty. The lights were off, and the closed sign on the door was flipped out. I had just stepped through the door, out into the windy street when Virginia came up behind me. She appeared to be on the verge of tears. She clutched my cell phone in one hand, like it was the last knot before the end of a rope.

"You left this," she said.

"I know."

She stared at me silently.

I looked at her a moment. "Do you need to tell me something?"

Her hands were shaking. She struggled to keep her voice steady as she spoke. "You're not the first man to come for Chelsea. A man came three days ago. I killed him."

Chapter Two

She offered to buy me a coffee, so I agreed to give her a few minutes of my time. I met her later that afternoon at a little diner called Elsie's. There was a shop on either side of it. One that sold an assortment of dolls and figurines hand-carved from wood, and the other, a clothing store that specialized in airbrushed t-shirts depicting phrases like, "Welcome to the Smokies," and "I Love Gatlinburg." The diner itself was far too clean. The sign out front was made to look like something you'd see dangling from a rusted pole along Route 66. But inside the floors had recently been mopped. A yellow "wet floor" sign stood just inside the entrance. The white-tiled walls seemed to glisten. We sat in a booth near the front window. Our table was wet from having been recently wiped down. You could smell cleanser in the air. It was just too clean.

A waitress wearing a white apron over a blue sundress took our order. Two coffees. Cream and sugar for Virginia. Extra cream and sugar for me. She left and came back a moment later with our coffees.

When the waitress had left our table, I said, "I'm not interested in getting in the middle of this."

"Then why did you agree to talk to me?"

I held up the coffee, took a sip.

"Let me at least explain," she said.

"I'll sip slowly," I said. "When I'm finished with this cup, I'm gone."

"He tried to kill Chelsea," she said. "The man who came before you. He broke into the bakery while Chelsea and I were sleeping upstairs. He came through the door with a knife, a mask over his face. I didn't give him a chance. I shot him." She said it in a single breath, her cup gripped tightly in one hand. She looked sick in the stark lighting of the diner. This had been weighing on her for some time.

"Sounds like you have a good case for self-defense," I said.

"I did," she said. She stared at the table, her cup gripped in both hands now. She raised it but didn't drink. Resting on her elbows, she let the cup float there over the table. "But I panicked." She looked at me. "Right after it happened, I didn't know what to do."

"Why didn't you call Lady Cop?" I said. I sipped my coffee. About half a cup left.

"Her name is Lindsay, and like I said, I panicked. Before a rational thought crossed my mind, Kyle and I had rolled the body up in a blanket and hurried it out the back door to his truck. We drove it to the highway, pulled over, and walked it a couple miles into the woods to the ravine."

"You're a limber old lady. Kyle's the cupcake guy?"

"Yes, Kyle works for me part time, and rents the room over the shop. I've been sleeping in there with Chelsea since she came to me a week ago."

"And now you can't claim self-defense because you've moved the body and failed to report the incident."

She set the cup down on the table, stared into it.

I took another sip of my coffee. I was down to the grounds now. I can do about four cups in a half hour.

"Does Lady Cop Lindsay know?" I said.

"I can't tell her," she said. She looked at me. "She'll want to cover for me. She'll end up losing her job over this, or get herself thrown in prison. All I've told her so far is that there was a man came by asking for Chelsea. I told her I saw him skulking around outside the bakery later that day, and that I thought James had something to do with it. I only told her that so she'd put a cop on watch at night."

"No one's found the body yet?"

"No. We hid it well. But someone will find it eventually."

I looked down into my cup. Coffee grounds floated in the last sip. A brown film laminated the interior of the cup. Not so clean after all. "What do you want me to do?" I said. I didn't look at her.

"I need you to prove Chelsea's father is trying to kill her." She watched the waitress shuffle past our table to an elderly couple that had just sat down. She sipped her coffee, then set it down and folded her hands in front of her mouth. She sat there like that a moment, eyes shut, as if in prayer. "I need you to go back to Charleston and find proof that James killed Chelsea's mother. My daughter. Chelsea saw it happen, and now he wants her dead too."

"How do you know all this?"

"Chelsea told me."

"Chelsea's a young girl. Maybe she's just upset that her mother died and this is a teen rebel kind of thing."

"Her mother didn't *die*. She was murdered."

"You said that already." I was finished with my coffee. "Even if you prove James killed Chelsea's mother, you'd probably still do time for putting this guy down."

"I'm concerned with Chelsea's safety," she said. "If you can save me in the process, that's just a bonus."

I looked out the window. The sidewalks were crowded now with tourists, and kids out of school for the weekend. A red neon sign that said "Bar" glowed above a dark doorway across the street. I knew where I was headed next. It would be that, and then back to the motel for the night. I had some thinking to do, and thoughts, to me, have always moved through a sober mind like sickle cells.

"Let me think about it," I said. And I got up and left her there.

The bar was themed, much like everything else in Gatlinburg. It seemed wherever you went around here they wanted you to feel like you were either in a log cabin during the early teens of the twentieth century, or in a gold mine in the mid to late nineteenth century. In the case of Bar, it was a ramshackle toss-up between the two.

When I had first walked in I'd felt the heat off the fire directly across the room. The fireplace had a tall, wide mouth, and though my initial suspicion had been it was gas and plastic logs, taking a seat at the end of the bar closest to it, I could see it was real. I hadn't noticed the smoke coming out of the top of the building, nor had I smelled it, and this had me worried I was itching a little more than usual.

"Help you?" the bartender said. He was out of sort with the rest of the place. A young guy, maybe late twenties. Thin, clean shaven, blond hair slicked back and stuck that way by some gunk he'd put in it. He looked at me like he knew me and was saddened by the choices I'd made in my life.

"Jack," I said, and held up three fingers. He looked at me, blinked twice. I took a clean glass from the stack just on the other side of the bar. Placed three fingers horizontally across the base of the glass. "Three fingers high," I explained, feeling even more like a drunk that I had to explain this to a bartender.

He smiled, as if we'd just shared an inside joke, and poured.

The bar wasn't crowded. Not for how busy it was outside. A couple tables of younger people, college age. Then the two or three gnarled guys you could swear are in every bar, slouched on their stools, an emptied glass pinched in a tight fist like a grenade with the pin removed. It was almost peaceful, how readily you could count on people to fail themselves the same way wherever you went. Or maybe I was just comforted to know I wasn't the only seasoned drunk in the room.

I was halfway through glass number two (four and a half fingers, give or take) when Lady Cop walked in. And I thought it that way when I saw her because I honestly couldn't remember her name.

"If it isn't Lady Cop," I said, feeling the pleasant heat of my breath passing over my lips. She stopped and gave me a look, thought, I could tell, to turn around and walk back out. But that would have been to give something up, to concede that I had gotten to her with my bigotry; and I saw she wasn't the type to give something up.

She walked over and sat on the stool right next to me. Put her elbows on the bar, facing the mirror behind it, and locked her fingers.

I looked at the bartender. "The usual for her," I said, grinning in a way I thought would be charming. When I'm drunk I think I'm charming.

He looked at me and blinked again. This guy wasn't going to make it. "Get her what she normally orders when she comes in here, and I will pay for it."

"I've never seen her before," he said.

"I don't come here," Lady Cop said. Lindsay was her name, I now remembered. She turned and looked at me, one elbow on the bar now, her other hand resting on her thigh. She was still wearing the black shoes, black slacks, and brown jacket. But she'd let her hair down. I didn't hate it.

"I don't drink," she said.

I made a show of scanning the room, as if to make sure we were in a bar. "Well, you're certainly not here for the pinball." I can be a bit of an asshole.

"I'm here to talk to you," she said.

I set my glass down, nodded to the bartender, who was still standing there staring at us, wondering what he should do. He refilled my glass. I picked it up as if to offer him a toast, said, "You might make it after all," to which he looked more confused than ever and went down the bar to serve a man who'd just walked in.

I set my glass down. "How'd you know I was here?"

"I know Aunt Virginia is fixed on getting you involved in whatever is going on with Chelsea and her father. I knew if I followed her this afternoon, she would lead me back to you."

"That's good detective work," I said, and finished off my glass. "But, as I mentioned earlier, I'm already involved in whatever is going on between Chelsea and her father, because her father hired me to bring her home."

She was silent a moment. "And I'm not so sure that's the worst thing that could happen," she said.

It was my turn to blink.

"I have no legal grounds to keep Chelsea from her father," Lindsay said. "She's a minor. Unless he has assaulted her or abused her in some way, Aunt Virginia is essentially her kidnapper. From all angles I can see this situation, her father is a man who has just lost his wife and now his daughter has run away from home. He's the victim, as far as I can tell."

"But why would Chelsea have run away?" I said. I wasn't certain the story Virginia had given me was true. I wasn't certain I wanted to get involved if it was. But the bartender had just refilled my glass, so I figured I would give this conversation a few more minutes.

"Her mother's death was traumatic for her, for all of us," Lindsay said. "And it's not just that she died, but how."

"How?"

She turned back toward the bar, leaned on her elbows and locked her fingers. "Virginia told me they found her washed up on shore right near where she and James live. She would go on these ill-advised night swims," she shook her head and went quiet.

"Were you close to Chelsea's mother?"

"Catherine," she said. "Her name was Catherine. Used to go to her house every summer when we were kids. A lot of weekends too. Back then she was Cat. After high school I went into the force and she got married and we lost touch."

"I'm sorry," I said, and it surprised me that I meant it. I was at a point in my life where feeling emotion, especially empathy, was surprising.

Lindsay turned her head just enough to give me a sidelong glare. But I saw that tenderness I'd detected earlier. "Do you even know what I'm saying?" she said, a half smile as she nodded toward my fifth glass, empty I realized. And yet here I sat—another surprise.

"You still haven't told me why you were looking for me," I said.

She looked across the bar into the mirror. "I feel like Aunt Virginia is keeping something from me."

"You think she'd tell me something she couldn't tell you?"

"I think she did." She didn't look over at me. Eyes on the mirror.

And I felt like I'd just allowed myself to be walked into a trap, shown the trigger, and happily sprung it on myself. I wasn't ready to get into the middle of this. I was, in fact, happy to head home and tell the judge of my failure, and continue to drink myself to death as I'd been doing before I'd taken this job. It had sounded so easy: pick up the girl and bring her home. Even had an address where I could find her. The judge could have easily hired a cab driver for two hundred dollars to do what I was tasked to do for two thousand. Yet here I was having been foiled by a grandmother, hanging around, indulging an attractive detective. Testing her, I realized. Underestimating her. Now I was curious what she knew about what I had been told. Despite myself, I was becoming curious about the truth of all this. I could feel the old cop in me stretching his tired limbs and glaring wide-eyed at his alarm clock.

But I knew better than to run with this feeling on first ring. If this case really wanted me, it would call again. If not, the feeling would pass, my interest would dissolve—as it usually did.

"She said she'd buy me a coffee, so I let her," I said.

"What did she tell you?" Still not looking at me. There was an energy to her stillness, a potential for action that left me wishing I'd had less to drink.

I thought about what I should say. One thing I knew about lying, the chief conceit, I guess, was that you sprinkle as few lies into your lie as possible. Give away enough of the truth so that you seem forthcoming, while disguising the rest in shrugged shoulders, raised eyebrows, and a general *I'm with stupid* demeanor.

The bartender came over and I placed my hand over top of my glass. He looked at me. "I'm good," I said, and he walked away. I turned to Lindsay. "Okay," I said, holding out my hand, as if the gift of my confession were cupped in my palm. "Granny seems to think that James had something to do with Catherine's death."

"She thinks James killed Cat?"

"Apparently that's what Chelsea told her."

I looked at Lindsay, and I didn't see the surprise I had expected to see on her face. Her face hardened, as if I'd just helped confirm a suspicion.

"You were thinking the same thing?" I said.

She stared at the bar a moment, then shook her head, looked up at me as if I'd just gotten back from the men's room. "James has always had anger issues," she said. "He's even seen a doctor about it."

"You think he could have snapped?"

She shook her head again. "I just can't see him doing that," she said. "He loved her and she loved him so much. I was at their wedding." She cupped her eyes in her hand a moment. "I remember being so jealous of how happy they looked."

"You think Chelsea's just acting out?"

"I can't see why she would," Lindsay said. "She's a smart girl, gifted classes, volunteers with her church. She wouldn't lie, and she's not one to act rashly or misplace blame."

"Her mother's never died before," I said. "Not to mention, she's thirteen years old. There is a certain level of immaturity that's just innate, only goes with age and experience. Maybe she's just not herself in her grief."

She shook her head again, slowly, and I couldn't tell anymore whether she was saying "no" or reorienting her thoughts.

"Chelsea wouldn't go this far on an emotional whim," she said. "At the very least, she believes James killed Cat. Whether or not it's true..."

"Looks like you've got some detective work to do," I said. I started to get up onto slightly unstable legs, and she grabbed me by the arm. And somehow I'd known she would do that. I had known I would get pulled into this situation since I'd seen Virginia staring out that window, contemplating my murder. The drunk in me wanted to shake her off and barrel out of there. But I sat back down, took a few breaths, and waited.

"You could get closer to him than I can," she said, giving me my arm back. She still wasn't looking at me.

"I suppose," I said.

"You could dig around, see if you can find any truth to what Chelsea's saying. If I go out there, he'll see right through me. I don't think I could hold back."

I looked at her now, and I couldn't have held back my grin if I'd been sober. "You suspected him from the start," I said.

"I've always suspected him," she said. "I knew this would happen. I just wish I'd done something about it."

"So why the dance?" I said. "Why not just come right out and ask me to snoop around?"

She looked at me now. "I didn't know who you were."

"And now you do?"

"I know you haven't walked away, though you want to and you could have. Why not?"

"I just tried to," I said.

But we both knew I hadn't tried very hard, and she didn't humor my comment with a reply. I looked at her a minute, knowing she knew, at least in part why I hadn't left yet. She'd run my I.D., surely checked my history. She knew I'd been a cop for twenty-five years. Any cop who's stuck to it long enough can tell you you never really turn it off, after a while. You see bad guys everywhere, and crimes are always occurring all around you, even when they're not. That old, atrophied cop inside me—he was a son of bitch, for sure. And I'd have shaken him off by now if I could have. I'd have kicked him before the drinking if given a choice. In my experience, he was a more dangerous habit.

What she said next told me she knew the other reason I'd stayed.

"I can get you paid for this, your normal rate, travel expenses. Whatever you need. If you'll do it."

I wasn't one to ask questions on any case where money was concerned (which was any case I took), and if you happened to peak my interest at the same time, you had me right where you wanted me. But I asked one now. "Why do you and Virginia so readily trust me, when a few hours ago you thought I was here to hurt Chelsea?"

She looked genuinely embarrassed. The thought that hiring me was unnecessary and potentially foolish had crossed her mind.

"I don't want to get the department involved until I have evidence," she said. "You're clean. And as I said, I always suspected James, and I get the feeling Chelsea is telling the truth. But if I accuse James now, or show him I'm suspicious, he'll lawyer up, and he'll wiggle his way out of this. He's smart. You're going back to him anyway. He knows you. He will let you into his house. I'm offering you a little money to go back there and tell him you failed. She wasn't at the bakery. Tell him you need more information to track Chelsea down." She turned on her stool, facing me. Ran a finger through a puddle of something on the bar top. "Get him to like you, maybe offer you another chance. Whatever you can do to have an excuse to ask questions, to be around his property."

I thought about it. "I am likeable."

A cell phone began to play Aerosmith's "Dream On," and she pulled it from her pocket and answered. She said a few words and hung up. Then she stood. "Think about it," she said as she tucked in her stool and headed for the door.

"What's up?"

"Couple of hikers just found a body in the woods off the highway."

I was staying at a cheap motel off the Parkway that stood along Baskins Creek. It was quiet and the creek was nice; and like I said it was cheap.

I put my key into the lock and lifted the door out of its haggard latch. The room was a confirmation of the saying, *you get what you pay for.* But it didn't bother me. Not the look of it, anyways. It was only the smell that concerned me. Cats. It took me back to my old Aunt Townsend on my mother's side, who'd lived the last years of her life as the stereotypical crazy cat lady down the street from my childhood home in North Charleston. Once cats spray, you might as well give the place over to them—you can't get that smell out with anything less than fire. And if you have a nose like mine, you'll have to bury the ashes.

I threw my jacket onto the bed and passed directly into the bathroom. I'd gotten used to the feel of the bandage on my head, not to mention I was fairly blitzed, and my reflection nearly caused me to leap back through the doorway. I approached the sink and touched the back of my head again. Still tender, but I thought now the bandage might have been overkill. I peeled back the adhesive tape over my forehead and unwound the bandage until my head was free. Ruffled, graying hair fell across my forehead, covering the red indentations left by the bandage. I touched the back of my head now. Blood on my fingertips. Might have had a concussion, though I didn't feel any special kind of dizzy or disoriented—just the kind I always felt after a few drinks. I thought maybe the drinking had been a bad idea all the same, having suffered a blunt force attack to the head severe enough to draw blood. But I also knew by experience that the drinking was inevitable, and had accepted long ago it would likely be the death of me.

I used the toilet, washed my face. I thought about shaving, but only as something I should try to remember to do tomorrow. I had an eight-hour drive to endure in the morning, and right now all I wanted to do was sleep.

I turned off the light and went back into the room. There was a chest in front of a vanity mirror next to a small TV. I took off my clothes in front of the mirror, and dropped them onto the chest with my shoulder holster on top. I looked at myself in the mirror, standing there in my boxers. Wavering slightly on my feet. I have broad shoulders, and a reasonably well-developed chest. I decided in my mid-thirties that I wasn't willing to do the work and make the sacrifices necessary to maintain a flat stomach, so I had resolved to build up my upper body to help disguise my inevitable gut while wearing clothes. It worked, for the most part, while wearing clothes.

I bent down, with effort, and removed my pistol from its holster. I carry a compact Smith and Wesson M&P Shield, 9mm. Not incredibly intimidating to look at, but it's lightweight, easy to conceal, and it does the trick. I stood there looking at myself in the mirror, holding my gun, and asked myself, out loud in a voice so clear and direct it sobered me up a second: "What do you think you're doing?"

And of course I was talking about this case. The fact I was considering taking it. The thing about me, I hadn't taken a case in years that might involve the least amount of danger, even less, exertion. Ever hear how people say being a P.I. isn't like in the movies? "It's not like *Magnum*," I've heard people say. Well, they're right. It's boring. That was always the appeal, to me. I did my time, served my community for twenty-five years. Took early retirement because, that's right, I couldn't stop drinking. Money got tight; so I got my Private Investigator's license and started doing contract work here and there—insurance companies, private citizens, courthouses. An occasional case like the one Tulley had offered me, a runaway kid who essentially needed a ride home. Other than that, whole days spent dozing in a car with a camera on some joker's front door.

Most danger I'd been in was a surveillance job on a farm out in Ladson, South Carolina. Lady was collecting disability due to a work related injury. The only out-of-sight place to post up was a line of trees about two acres off from the house, just inside her property line. I was lying there with an expensive high-zoom camera braced across a fallen tree, watching, when her Doberman walked up. I lied there, waiting to die, and the dog sniffed my hair and walked off. That's the closest I'd come to excitement in this job.

And now I was considering getting involved in a murder investigation. I'd dealt with murder cases to an extent during my years as a patrolman. Usually when I responded to a dispatch, the perp was gone from the scene. I'd cordon off the area, handle crowd control until the detective arrived. He'd ask me questions, and later, gather my report into a file. Meanwhile, I was back on patrol, responding to the next call. I'd never gone for the detective position, though it had been suggested I try for it. I'd always liked the freedom of being a patrolman, the ability to let go of one case and move on to the next. I went home at night free of responsibility. But I had loved being a part of the solution. I'd taken a great deal of satisfaction from the knowledge that I had helped put a killer away. And I guess now it was that part of me, that cop, still alive but the worst kind of groggy, rubbing his eyes with a *How long was I out* look on his face, that gave me the idea I could pull this off.

Dominic Stabile

I needed the money. That was first, I think. I could not say no to a job these days. With Google and Facebook, people barely need P.I.s anymore. But the scary thing, and I thought this just before I fell straight back onto the bed and passed out, was that I felt some pull from this case. I wanted it. Some last-ditch effort to prove myself, I guess. And I thought I'd gotten past all that long ago.

Chapter Three

I made three stops on my way back to Charleston. Mostly to take Aspirin or to piss. But the trip took me closer to nine hours. When I got there I went straight to my North Charleston apartment and dug out the bottle of Maker's Mark I keep in the little cabinet over the stove. I grabbed a shot glass, filled it and pulled. I did four more, put the bottle away, and dropped into my bed. I slept four hours. The sleep was fitful, and I had strange dreams I can't remember the details of. My dreams usually have to do with my late wife, Nancy, so I assume they were on that topic. I know they were uncomfortable dreams, so it seems likely.

When I got up, I felt worse than when I'd arrived. My tongue was stuck to the roof of my mouth, and I felt like someone had rapped a cotton blanket around my brain and closed my skull over it. I stumbled to the kitchen and stuck my head under the faucet, catching the lukewarm water in my mouth, spitting hangover gunk into the sink.

I put on a new button down shirt, slipped my beige jacket over it, and headed out. I'd decided to read a paper, and I knew where Catherine, or Cat, had been found dead. According to the article, Cat had gone out for her usual nightly swim. She and James had had some sort of fight, and he'd gone straight to bed. He'd woken up the next day to find the bed empty.

When she hadn't turned up by the afternoon, he'd called the police, and they'd eventually located her body, tangled up in the legs of the pier. I thought I'd start on the pier, see what I could kick up.

The judge had himself a nice little beach house. So nice, in fact, that the beach itself was considered private, though plenty of people could be found out there any given day, and the homeowners rarely made it an issue. I parked off the main road a few houses down from the judge, and slipped between two beach houses and out to the area where Cat had been found.

It was late afternoon, and ten degrees warmer here than it had been in Tennessee. But there was a nice breeze, and it was cool enough that I didn't feel too out of place, sloshing through the sand in my slacks and jacket. I didn't see anyone down the beach in either direction.

I walked onto the pier and stood there looking out at the ocean a moment. The horizon was almost black, where night had already come to places farther east. Subtle waves made a fuss and died against the pier. I stood there feeling comforted, for some reason I don't understand. Maybe there's something to the whole fresh air thing, I don't know. I enjoyed that a moment, and then turned to face the judge's house. He was three houses down from the pier, making the pier a total of maybe a hundred yards from where Cat would have most likely entered the water. I'm not a genius—I'll be the first to tell you that every time. But a thought came to me then I couldn't shake. And that thought was, when most people drown they don't turn up so close to where they went into the water—at least not in the ocean. The whole reason you drown is the current gets a hold of you, drags you out to sea, and before you know it your feet don't touch the ground anymore and you go under, and the sea sets you down somewhere miles away once it's bored of you.

But Cat had turned up right here. Right below my feet. Drown a hundred yards from her home, in a stretch of water she'd presumably swam for years. Her own little therapy. Most people would say a healthier form of therapy than my own; but whiskey hadn't killed me yet.

The next thing I noticed was that part of the railing had broken away. I looked over the edge, watched the waves shatter against the legs of the pier. Falling off wouldn't be a certain death sentence, but it wasn't my idea of a good time either.

I was turning to head back, when the sun, still hanging over the roofs of the beach houses opposite the ocean, glinted off something wedged between two cracked boards in the pier floor. I crouched down and plucked it out. A gold watch. I turned it over, but there was nothing etched on the underside. No initials. No "To JT with love." Trust me, it's never that easy. But one thing I've learned is to treat everything like it's the final piece of the puzzle. With that thought I slipped the watch into the pocket of my jacket and headed toward the judge's house.

He must have seen me coming. He met me on the back patio in a pair of high-riding blue shorts and a short-sleeved button down covered in green palmetto trees. If you don't know, the palmetto tree became a part of the SC state flag because someone had the idea to use palmetto logs for the walls of Fort Moultrie back in the civil war. Canon balls bounced right off because the wood has give, almost like rubber. I was about to test Tully's own resilience myself, see what bounced back.

He set his drink—good scotch, no doubt—on the porch railing and squinted down at me as I climbed the steps. He looked like he was trying to talk, but he had to catch the words with his lips first, and they were slippery.

I held up a hand in a gesture I hoped was calming, and said, "I know, I know. I can explain. But first, can I get one of those?" I nodded toward his glass.

"You show up out of the blue without my daughter, and you ask me for a drink?"

"I said I can explain," I said. He backed up to let me onto the porch. I was bent over, hands on my knees. I was trying to get a full breath, but it had been a few years since I'd done an eight minute mile, or done a mile at all, for that matter. And whatever good I'd felt out on the pier had left me during my walk over here.

"What happened?" he said.

I stood up straight, getting my wind back now. "She wasn't there," I said.

"You went to the bakery?"

I nodded. "Met granny. Nice old lady."

"Did you check her house?"

"What?"

"Virginia? She doesn't live at the bakery. She could easily be hiding Chelsea at her house."

"I checked the house," I said. "What do you think I am?"

"I think you're a drunk," he said. "That's what Kim told me—after I hired you, of course. She called me up a day too late, like her conscience was bothering her."

"Kimmy told you I'm a drunk?" I said, just buying myself time to think. It sounded like Kimmy, all right. She was always throwing jobs my way, trying to keep me busy. But the jobs were normally the boring stuff, surveillance and all that—you'd be amazed how many people divulge their intimate problems to bartenders. I guessed she threw me this one because she knew I was in a bad spot, behind on rent, but never to be caught without a bottle in the cabinet. Then she got nervous, wondering whether or not I could handle it. I'd talk to her later. Let her know if she was taking it upon herself to be my therapist, she might learn a little about confidentiality.

"Yes, she did," Tully said, pacing around the porch now, running a hand through his hair. He stopped and looked at me. "What did Virginia say when you asked her about Chelsea?"

"She looked genuinely baffled," I said

He stared at me a moment, searching for a tell. But I've got a pretty good poker face.

He shook his head and turned away, pacing again now. He took his drink from the railing and sipped at it.

"Why don't we talk inside?" I said. "I'm getting sand in my teeth out here."

He stopped with his back to me, as if I'd snapped him with a wet towel. Then he passed through the sliding glass door to the house and left it open behind him.

It felt good to get out of the wind. I spotted an end table just before the kitchen. There was a cordless phone and a framed photo of Tully with an attractive woman that must have been his late wife. He had passed into the next room. I slipped the gold watch from my pocket and tucked it back behind the phone dock, like it might have fallen there. Then I followed him into the expansive living room.

White carpet. White sofa. Fifty inch TV. He made his way to the bar across the room, refreshed his drink, and turned to me.

"I'll get you the cash tomorrow, for your trouble," he said, staring into his glass. "I guess I'll have to go get her myself."

"I'm telling you she's not there," I said. I moved toward the sofa and took a seat on the arm. "But I want to find her for you."

He looked up at me and then back into his glass. He took a sip. "I don't think so," he said. "I don't want my daughter riding in a car with you anyways."

That comment surprised me. If I was to believe Virginia and Lindsay, this guy was out to kill his daughter to keep her quiet. If I got behind the wheel drunk and did it for him, all the better, right?

"Listen," I said. "I got a problem, but I don't drive drunk."

"For all I know you never left town," he said.

He finished his drink and went back to the bar. He had his back to me a moment, then he turned with a fresh drink, walked down the single step into the living room and sat on the sofa opposite me. He looked tired, and more than that— depressed. Deeply depressed. It was almost the same way he'd looked the last time I'd spoken to him. When I'd seen him three days earlier, I had seen a man torn up with loss. Looking at him now, I saw a man torn up with loss who'd spent the last three days drinking expensive stuff.

"I just want to get my daughter back," he said, and he looked up at me, his eyes shining. "I know she's hurting." He looked down into his glass. "And there are things she doesn't understand."

"What sorts of things?" I said.

"Personal things," he said without raising his head. "I truly hoped you would come through for me."

"The amount of times I've heard that," I said, slipping off the arm of the couch and onto the plush cushion. "Though normally it's a woman saying it."

He looked at me now, and his expression would have been the same had he been watching a watermelon explode in super slow-motion. "You find humor in everything, don't you?"

"Honestly, no," I said. "Everyone who knows me says I mope too much."

He exhaled a harsh breath through clinched teeth, shook his head and went back to his drink. It's against my religion, but I was starting to feel sorry for him.

"Jokes aside," I said. "All I need's a little more info, and I can get your girl back for you."

"Info?" he said. "You mean besides where she's located?"

"Info like, why'd she run off in the first place?"

He looked at me for a long time, and I'll admit, I worried he was seeing right through me. But then he looked away and said, "She thinks her mother's death was my fault."

"How so?"

"That's the personal part. And how is knowing that going to help you find my daughter, who is not lost, but simply away? All I needed you to do was put her in a car and drive her here. No detective work required."

"You might be wrong about that," I said.

"Why's that?" he said.

"Because this 'personal' stuff you keep referring to might be something I could pass on to Chelsea for you. If I knew what went on here, what she was feeling, I might be able to get her to trust me."

"Won't do you any good if you can't find her," he said. "And anyways, she wouldn't believe you. Not as long as she knows I sent you." He set his drink on an end table and took a pack of cigarettes from his shirt pocket. He coaxed one out, put it between his lips and lit it. He exhaled a plume of smoke and watched it disappear.

"You never know," I said. "Kids love me."

"There you go with that humor again," he said. He leaned forward onto his knees. "Can I ask you a question?"

His tone told me the question would likely be rhetorical, but I nodded anyway.

"Do I have a smile on my face?" he said.

I nodded and got to my feet. "If you change your mind, you have my card."

"I destroyed your card the instant I found out you were a bumbling idiot."

"I'll assume that's the drink talking," I said. I took one of my business cards out of my wallet and set it on the end table next to the sofa. "In case you feel differently in the morning."

"I won't," he said.

I shrugged. "If that's the way it is."

"It is," he said, moving to walk me out the front door.

"Actually, I'll go the back way, if you don't mind. I was enjoying the view earlier."

I headed back toward the patio and he followed behind me to see me out. I made it a point to look casually toward the end table by the kitchen as I passed by.

"Nice watch," I said, taking the gold watch from its spot behind the phone dock. "I've been looking to get a new one. How much did this run you?"

He reflexively gripped his right wrist in his left hand, and I noticed the three scratch marks there for the first time.

"Where did you get that?" he said.

"Right there," I said, nodding toward the end table.

He stared at it a moment, and his lips did that thing again, like words kept slipping out of their grip before he could bite down on them.

"That's not mine," he said, more to himself than to me.

"Well, it was in your house, on your end table," I said, holding it out to him. I tried on a big smile.

He looked at me, his face turning red; and for a second I thought he was going to slug me. But he blinked a few times, took another sip of his drink, and then took the watch. He examined it a second, and then said, "I guess it is mine. I thought I'd lost it."

"When was that?" I said.

"When was what?" he said.

"The day you lost it."

"Some time ago, now." He grinned. "I don't know the exact day."

"Seems like you would," I said.

"And why is that?"

I paused and watched his face. His jaw flexed, and his eyes seemed to look past me and into a dismal future. "It would be the last day you knew what time it was," I said.

He let out another of his pinched laughs, more of a sigh than anything else. He guided me out the back door into the windy evening.

As I left him and walked back down the beach toward the pier, itching for a drink, I thought about what Lindsay and

Virginia had said about him, their accusations. And it was true, he was quick to anger, and a power junky to boot. But I was going to need more than that before I could get the local PD involved.

Chapter Four

Kimmy ran a little bar off King Street. Sort of my second home. It was dark by the time I pushed through the door and took my usual seat at the end of the bar. Kimmy was leaned over the bar top, staring down at a sheet of paper on which another regular—a homeless guy some of the younger patrons called "Dirty Santa" on account of his white beard—was drawing something. She watched patiently a moment, dirty rag slung over her shoulder, soft chin resting in a rough hand, as her eyes wandered. Kimmy was a dreamer, and I had warned her about that almost as often as she had warned me about my alcoholism.

When she saw me, she patted Santa on the shoulder, told him he was quite the artist, and walked over to me with a pensive look on her face. Did I mention that face was gorgeous? That it swam up through the fog of my dreams some nights, and I'd wake up with my lips still tingling, and my boxers not fitting quite right? Well, there you have it.

"A spaceship," she said, her chiseled expression braking only enough for her mouth to shape the words.

I watched her patiently, with no small amount of adoration showing on my face. She brought my dreams and she brought my drinks. I really had a crush on this girl.

"That's what he's drawing," she said. She yanked the rag from her shoulder and began scrubbing the bar top with it. "Santa is drawing me a picture of the spaceship he's building, which he needs to escape the imminent rise of 'robot communism.'" She stopped scrubbing the bar top, filled a shot glass with Jack, and set it in front of me. She gave me a heartbroken look and said, "What could that even be?"

I shot the Jack and set the glass back on the bar top. "Having another existential crisis?"

She slumped forward, resting on her elbows. "I keep thinking, I graduated college ten years ago, you know?"

She refilled my glass. I put two fingers on the rim, but didn't drink it right away, trying to pace myself.

"That's not so bad," I said. "Plenty of people are still finding themselves at thirty-two."

She rolled her eyes at me and stood up straight. "You know I graduated at twenty-five, right?"

I shot my second drink and slid the glass toward her. I smiled. "Plenty of people are still finding themselves at thirty-five."

She hit me with the rag and turned to help a customer farther down the bar. But I could see the little smile on her face. When I could do that, it was a good day.

While she was busy, I scanned the room for familiar faces. But I didn't see anybody I knew. Kimmy's place was a dump, if I'm being honest. But it had its charm. It was just the right kind of dark and tucked away, you know? You go to a bar alone, you're hiding. Maybe you tell yourself you're looking to hook up with someone, shoot the shit with a stranger; but you know the world's outside. That's where your family and friends are if you have any. That's where your job is if you have one. If anyone is going to miss you or cry to see you go, they're outside that bar. But there you are, slouched over a drink, not talking to anybody. You're hiding. And this place was the right kind of dark for it. I spent most of my days hiding there, sometimes thinking Kimmy might look to me as someone she wanted to take home, but usually just looking for quiet, a place to step off the track and let the other runners blow by with all the blind hope and motivation and will I didn't have anymore.

After a minute, Kimmy came back over and poured me another drink.

"So, how'd the job go?"

I took the shot before I answered. "I'm getting paid."

"You don't sound happy about it."

I shrugged, trying to look casual. "Tully got the idea I'm not reliable," I said.

She looked down at the bar a moment, chewing her lip. "Listen, I just got to thinking about the girl, and I tried to imagine you going eight hours without stopping for a drink and—"

I put up a halting hand. "Don't apologize," I said, but it didn't come out as softly as it sounded in my head. "I haven't given you any reason to think anything different."

She looked at me without blinking for long enough that I became uncomfortable. I slid the glass toward her, and that seemed to snap her out of it. "I'm sorry," she said as she filled the glass. "You know I think the world of you. I just felt responsible. I referred you, you know?"

I nodded and took the shot. "On a side note, I'm still on the case, in a way."

"In what way?" She went to fill the glass again and I put my hand over it. I'm not sure why, as I knew I'd let her fill it up again in a minute.

"I found the girl," I said. "Got the knot on my head to prove it. She and her grandma are scared. The whole family is, in fact."

"Scared of what?"

"Tully," I said, lowering my voice a little. "They've got it in their heads that the judge killed his wife, and that's why the girl ran off. She swears she saw it happen."

"Jesus," Kimmy said, leaning closer.

"I visited the judge today when I got back. He wasn't happy I came empty handed."

"I bet not," she said.

I told her about the watch, and his reaction to it.

"So you think he did it?"

"I don't know what to think yet," I said. "On the one hand, the guy's an asshole, and he seems like the type to get a little wound up and do something violent before he knows what's happened. On the other hand, I got the feeling he's genuinely worried about his girl."

"But couldn't that just be because she's got his life in her hands, being a witness to the murder he committed?"

"That's a thought," I said. "But it doesn't feel that way."

"What are you going to do?" she said.

"I'm heading over to talk to Parker. See if he knows anything about the judge."

I slid the shot glass toward her. She refilled it.

"And of course I'm going to go to the funeral," I said. "It's tomorrow."

"What are you going to do there? Go around with a flip pad questioning the mourners?"

"See who shows up," I said. "If James and Cat were having problems, chances are someone there will know about it." I took the shot. "I'll need a date, of course. And you know Tully."

"I took a business law class he taught once ten years ago."

"And you got me in contact with him in the first place. It won't look right if I show up alone."

She shook her head, but I saw her mouth curving up to one side. Her eyes sparkling. "It's too late notice to get a sitter for Jeffy."

"Bring him," I said, and she hit me with the rag again.

Parker was a young reporter for a local newspaper called the *Holy City Horn*. It was mostly an e-zine that occasionally released a pamphlet that looked like the sort of thing you'd find tucked behind the flag of your mailbox. I hated everyone who worked for the paper, including Parker. They found problems where there were none, and most of their rag was speculation borrowed from obvious major articles of other papers—the one percent this, the conservatives that. I didn't know anything much about politics other than I didn't want to know anything much about it. But Parker and his friends prided themselves on knowing everything about everyone in a certain income bracket, and that was one thing they had going for them.

They ran their operation out of the college. Parker was a grad student there, and he taught part time and edited his little zine. When I walked into the office they used a couple days a week, he was at a computer, staring at the screen. With his heavy-framed glasses and his twenty-years-too-late bowl cut, he looked like an owl trying to interpret scripture.

He didn't notice me until the door snapped shut. By then I was standing next to him.

He looked up. "Nick? I didn't hear you come in."

"You should be more alert. If I was a corporate assassin come to silence the young, Marxist interloper, you'd have been dead before you got that Pulitzer."

"Hilarious," he said.

"What are you working on so intently over here?"

"You know about the demolition going on off King?"

"Which one?"

"The old library," he said.

"It's a dump," I said. "Not to mention, old news."

"It's a part of the local culture," he said. "It was anyway. Now it's going to be a Holiday Inn."

"People need a place to sleep," I said. "What they don't need is one more rotten building sagging over the street."

"Your office is in one of those sagging buildings," he said, and he had me there.

"Fair enough," I said. "But that's my office." I rolled a chair up to his desk and sat down. "What do you know about James Tully?"

"You don't even want to know the angle I'm taking?"

"Were the rats living in the old book stacks of an endangered variety?"

"Forget it."

"Okay."

"James Tully?" he said, typing something on his keyboard. He read what popped up. "Local judge. Family man. Graduated Cum Laude from Ole Miss in '93. You know, Google works from any computer with internet access."

"I need to know things Google might not have just yet," I said. "The kind of stuff you and your friends with the picket signs glued to their hands would know."

Parker continued reading a moment, then said, "He looks clean. If he hasn't done anything newsworthy, we wouldn't have had any reason to look into his life."

"You think you can look into his life for me?"

"Why?"

"I got a client who thinks he might have killed his wife."

"Oh, I see it," he said. "She died just last week. It says she drown."

"That's what the judge says."

"You think he's lying?"

"I've seen the coroner's report—she drown. But I have reason to believe she had help."

"Give me some time," he said. "I'll call you if I find anything."

I got up. "Thanks. And don't go publishing anything until I get some facts together."

"I wouldn't do that," he said.

"No, never," I said, and left.

Chapter Five

The next morning I still hadn't heard back from Parker. I popped five Aspirin with a liter of water, first thing. It's become an almost comforting ritual. I took a long shower, which I desperately needed, threw on my only decent suit, and headed for Kimmy's house. She lived off Cosgrove in an area that seemed to hang over its own hopeless future like a beach house over an eroding shoreline. If nature didn't reclaim the spaces where the squat, rotting houses currently stood, capitalism would plant a shopping center there soon enough.

She was out the door before I even pulled in. I came to a sudden stop, and the car rocked as I watched her approach. Slim black dress, conservative in length, but with a revealing fabric that kicked the humble flower idea out the nearest window. The girl could work the color black.

She grinned when she saw me staring, rolled her eyes. She got into the passenger seat and cupped her hands under my chin, as if collecting my sagging tongue to place it back in my mouth. Her sense of humor was one of many things I'd grown to love about her. I laughed, and she rolled her eyes again and buckled her seat belt.

Banging on my window.

My head spun so fast I nearly pulled a muscle. But it was just the boy, Jeffy. Nine years old, and smarter than I was; I'd known him since he was three, and that had always been the case. He currently wore the wide-eyed, anxious look of a kid who wants to come too.

I rolled down the window.

"Whatcha say, kiddo?"

"Where are you guys going?" he said.

I looked at Kimmy, and she nodded.

I turned to Jeffy. "Funeral," I said.

"You're gonna go look at dead people?"

"A dead person," I said.

"Is it your mom?"

"No," I said. "I don't know her."

"You don't know your mom?"

"No, my mom was an angel. I don't know the dead lady."

"Then why are you going?"

I looked at Kimmy. She shrugged.

"Respect," I said, smiling at the kid. Kimmy let out a sarcastic, *ha!*

"You respect her, but you didn't know her?"

"Yes?"

He looked thoughtful and unsatisfied with my answer. "You're lying," he said.

"And if you were old enough to work, I'd know just the job for you," I said.

He looked confused. Kimmy spoke up: "Aunt Maggie came all the way over here just to play with you. Do you want to hurt her feelings?"

He shook his head.

"Mommy will be back in a couple of hours, okay?"

He nodded and ran back into the house.

"He's cute," I said.

"He's a demon," she said.

"You look nice," I said.

"This is weird," she said.

Whiskey for Breakfast

"Well, stick around," I said, and we were on our way.

The attendees of Cat's funeral were some of the higher elect in Charleston. I could see that just by the cars in the parking lot. I might as well have been handing the valet the reigns of a horse-drawn carriage, the way he looked at me when I handed him the keys to my '96 Taurus. And, no, there was not actually a valet there taking keys.

We entered the church and took a seat in back. I spotted Tully and his closer relatives up on the front row. And I thought then, either he was a great actor or he was being falsely accused, the way he sobbed. Of course, there was also the possibility he was suffering guilt. Most murders that occur between spouses are sudden, violent outbursts that get out of control. I knew he could have killed Cat, regretted it immediately. Then, once he saw there was nothing he could do, he covered it up as best he could. Back when I was a cop, I'd once responded to a domestic violence call. A husband and wife had been arguing, and then the neighbor had heard a gunshot. When I arrived, the husband was on his knees next to his wife's dead body, crying and trying to put her brains back in.

The point is I didn't know what to think yet. But Tully knew more than he was saying. That I would have bet real money on.

After the service, the pallbearers carried the casket out into the cemetery around back of the building. We followed the solemn congregation, and I did my best to stay out of Tully's view until I was ready to talk.

The path we walked sloped up a fairly steep hill and then leveled off. Cat's plot was there, in a little stretch of earth before the path sloped back down, more gradually, and fed into a field of gravestones. They had set up a cloth pavilion, and Tully and the older mourners took the seats beneath it, while the rest of us stood outside of it, looking in as the priest said a few more words. Before long the body was lowered into the ground, and everyone got to their feet and there was a general murmur about a reception, and finger foods. I found myself wondering absently if drinks would be served.

"He looks pretty broken up for a murderer," Kimmy said. She had a little black pocketbook to match her dress. It had a silver, chain-link strap, and she kept adjusting it, sliding the strap up to the crook of her elbow, and then back down to her wrist. She looked uncomfortable.

"My thoughts exactly," I said. "Although he could just be a good actor."

"There's that," she said. "I guess I should go pay my respects." She started toward the pavilion.

The mourners were lining up under the pavilion to offer their condolences to James. Then they were heading down the hill toward the reception hall. I stayed near the back of the group, avoiding eye contact. I wanted to speak to James alone when the time came, in case he wasn't so happy to see me crashing his wife's funeral. In the interim, I planned to watch anyone who looked particularly upset. Anyone who might have been close enough to the Tully family to know their secrets.

A young blonde approached James, maybe mid-twenties, and he excused himself from the gathered friends and family and guided her away, jabbing his finger at her as they spoke heatedly. He wasn't happy to see her.

"Excuse me."

I turned to see an elderly woman looking up at me. She was leaning on a metal cane with a plastic handle, and used her other hand to dry her eyes.

"Yes?" I said. I looked around to make sure I kept Tully within view. He was still arguing with the blonde. Most of the congregation was moving down the hill.

"I saw you yesterday," the woman said. I turned back to her. "You were behind my house."

I tried to remember what I had done after leaving the bar last night. "That right?" I said. "Listen, if I damaged any property, I'll pay for it."

"I'm not sure what you mean," she said. "I saw you walking on the beach behind my house yesterday, and you were speaking with James."

"Oh, right," I said. "So?"

"You're the private investigator he hired to find little Chelsea?"

I nodded. "I thought that was a bit of a secret."

"Word gets around," she said.

"I guess it does," I said.

She looked at me a second, then she said, "I live two houses north of James."

I looked at her, trying to figure out the significance. Then it hit me. "Gives you a pretty good view of the pier, doesn't it?"

She looked down, then up beyond me to where Tully stood. Her face turned two shades, and fresh tears set her eyes shining. "It does," she said. "But I don't want to talk about anything here. It's sacrilegious."

I took a business card from my wallet, handed it to her. "That's the address and number to my office. I'll be there this afternoon."

She tucked the card into a pocketbook hanging from her arm. She shook her head and looked sullen. Then she looked up at me, nodded, shrugged, and then followed the other mourners back down the hill toward the reception hall.

I saw that Kimmy was already on her way down, her left arm hooked around James' right as he continued to put on an award-winning performance. The blonde was gone.

The door to the church's social hall opened into a small foyer, lined with portraits of the numerous priests who had presided over the congregation. Grim, stoical men. The most recent portrait showed a "Father Beaumont, 2005 – present."

Only he wasn't the one who had given the sermon today, or said the final prayers before Cat was lowered into the ground. The one who had done that was two portraits back. "Father O'Neil, 1990 – 2000." In his portrait he looked taller, though he was only visible from the waist up. The shading of his face lent him a gaunt, haunted quality. A quality nowhere to be found in the plump, jovial man I'd seen today. The man who now stood at the food table along the back wall of the expansive hall, filling a white, plastic plate with quiche.

From the look of the hall, and the sparks of laughter that rose out of the general murmur like gun shots, I could have been at a wedding reception. White cloths lay over small tables. Cylindrical light fixtures hung from the ceiling, giving off a warm glow no more pervasive than candle flames. The ceiling was vaulted, and running up through the peak was a stained glass window. Sunlight made kaleidoscopic shapes along the dark wooden planks of the ceiling. I found myself scanning the tables for champagne. But this was going to be a dry affair.

James stood just outside the foyer, hands folded in front of him as guests continued to offer their condolences. I slipped past him and moved among the cloth-covered tables toward Father O'Neil. I figured if he was doing Cat's funeral instead of the current priest, maybe he was close to the Tully family, doing them a favor for old time's sake. But someone gripped my arm and spun me around.

"Where have you been?" Kimmy said. She was holding a plate of finger foods, still trying to decide on the right place to hang her pocketbook.

"I made a new friend," I said.

"You left me alone," she said.

"You left me."

"I had to say *something* to him," she said, and I could tell she was agitated.

"What did he say?"

She took a deep breath, shook one hand in the air as if she'd just dipped her fingers in boiling water. "He could barely get a word out. I just kept telling him it was going to be okay. But he's inconsolable. He was going on and on about Chelsea. And how he's all alone now. I don't know. It didn't look like acting to me."

I looked over at James. He was nodding his head to each person who approached him, but you could tell his mind wasn't there. He had the look of a man lost in suffering, or lost in plotting. I still wasn't sure which. But I knew that look. I'd worn it myself. At this thought I looked down at the wedding band on my own finger. I'd begun twirling it with the opposite hand, a nervous habit I'd formed at some point that often left a raw loop in my skin just below the knuckle. Kimmy saw me doing it, and I quickly shoved my hands into my pockets.

"So you don't think he could have done it?" I said.

She shook her head, but looked at me another moment. I noticed then the way she'd done her hair. She'd drawn most of it up into a loose bun, and blond ribbons trailed down either side of her face, framing it like a picture. Something about the warm lighting of the room gave her a regal quality I hadn't noticed out in the daylight. I liked it, and I felt a little guilty thinking about her that way in the middle of this conversation, standing under stained glass.

"I honestly don't think he did it," she said.

I nodded. "The thing is, I've got three people telling me not only did he do it, but he's been the type of man to do something like it his whole life."

"Are these people reliable?"

"One's his daughter. She's thirteen, and I had reservations about taking her word for it. Thought she might just be acting out over the death of her mother. But then the grandmother was so insistent. She's backing the girl all the way. And then Chelsea's aunt is a cop, and she's the one who says James has had a bad temper all along. That she always feared that Cat's death at his hand was only a matter of time."

"He could have been an asshole his whole life," Kimmy said. "That doesn't mean he did it. He obviously loved her a lot."

"He could have loved her a lot," I said. "That doesn't mean he didn't do it."

Kimmy shook her head, plucking a slice of pineapple from her plate and placing it in her mouth. "I just don't see it," she said, chewing the fruit. "That's my professional opinion."

"Professional?" I said. "I'm the investigator, remember?"

"And I'm the bartender. I know a bullshit story when I see it." She jabbed a finger in James' direction. "That's no bullshit, I'm telling you."

I stood there a moment, thinking about whether or not I should say what I wanted to say next. Then I said it. "Someone tried to kill Chelsea."

She stared a moment, chewing. She swallowed before she spoke. "Someone?"

"The girl and the grandmother saw him enter the house, mask over his face and knife in hand."

"What happened?"

I looked at her a second. "Grandma shot him. Now I've got to prove James sent this thug to take Chelsea out, otherwise Grandma might do hard time. She might do time anyways. But that's the job."

"You said the girl's aunt is a cop. Does she know about the guy with the knife?"

"She knows someone was skulking around, and she knows Grandma and Chelsea suspect James sent him. But she doesn't know Grandma shot the guy. Not yet."

She thought a moment. "But what if James really didn't send him?"

"Then my job gets harder," I said. "I'll have to find out who did."

Whiskey for Breakfast

I glanced over toward the food table. Father O'Neil wasn't there. I scanned the room, spotted him exiting a side door with his plate of food. "I'll catch up with you," I said, starting toward him. I stopped and turned back. "You might be right about James, but I have to follow where the evidence takes me. Right now, he's it."

"You're leaving me again?" I heard her say, as I moved toward the door.

The door led to a small park. The earth was sandy where the grass had been stomped out by years of daycare kids. Three towering oaks made a canopy of gnarled branches, which hung over a jungle jim, a tall metal slide, and a rusty roundabout. Father O'Neil had taken a seat on a picnic table in the shade and was facing away from me, toward a small pond at the back of the property.

"Quieter out here," I said, as I approached.

It took him a second to turn on his seat. He squinted at me, decided he didn't recognize me, but smiled anyway. "I always loved it out here," he said.

"Loved?" I said, playing dumb. If I got him talking about himself, he might be more open to my questions.

"I used to preach here," he said, eating a round of quiche with his fingers. He smiled. "That was an age ago, now."

"You mind?" I said, gesturing toward the bench across from him.

"Not at all."

I sat down. "You retire?"

"I had health issues," he said, looking at me. Up close he looked older. Gray wisps of hair moved in the wind, and I could see some of that haunted quality from the portrait in the sag of his eyes and the slight wrinkle of concern on his brow. "Throat cancer. Nearly killed me. It didn't, obviously, but it's hard to give voice to the word of God when you can't speak."

"You ever think God was trying to tell you something?" I said. I meant it as a joke, but I immediately wondered if I'd crossed a line.

His smile was disarming. "More than once," he said, and the smile stayed as he turned his eyes back toward the pond. "I was away for so long by the time I had my voice back, I decided to stay away. But I came back today as a friend of James and Catherine Tully." He looked at me. "What's your relation to the deceased?"

"I'm here with a friend," I said. "I mean, she knew James and wanted to offer her support. I'm supporting her."

He was still smiling, but it was less disarming now. There was something in it. The look in his eyes had changed too. They weren't lax anymore. They were keen, alight with curiosity. "You followed me out here," he said. "Why?"

"Just came to get some fresh air," I said.

He nodded, slowly, then went back to his quiche.

"Though, I would like to ask you a few questions, if you don't mind."

He shook his head, smiled again. "I don't mind. Are these questions concerning God?"

"No," I said.

"And why not?" he said. He turned completely on the bench now, swinging his feet under the table. "Can I ask you a question first?"

"You just did," I said.

He watched me with that smile on his face, and suddenly I felt like my Catholic schoolboy self again, eleven years old and having just dropped the F-bomb during the dismissal prayer. "Sure," I said. "Go ahead."

"When was the last time you went to confession?"

"I couldn't tell you."

"But you are a man of faith?"

I looked at him. I didn't like where this conversation was going. "I used to be," I said, "an age ago, now."

Whiskey for Breakfast

He ate another piece of quiche, looked at me until he was done chewing. "In my experience, men who say they have lost their faith have simply replaced God with something else." He nodded toward the table.

I hadn't realized it, but I had set my right hand on the table. I looked down at it. I had gotten so used to the shakes, I didn't even think to hide it anymore. It usually happened anywhere from three to eight hours after my last drink. I was going on fourteen hours now. I took my hand off the table and set it in my lap.

"I had a brother who used to drink whiskey at breakfast," he said. He was looking at his plate now, picking up hunks of quiche and putting them in his mouth. "He did it so he could get by to lunch. Then, at lunch, he went out for more drinks. This way he could get through the work day. At five, he hit the bar, and he was usually there until he went to bed." He looked up at me. "The longest he ever went without drinking was the hours he spent sleeping. He would wake up with the shakes. So, he would drink whiskey for breakfast."

"My mother always said if you drink before noon you're an alcoholic," I said.

"And do you?" he said.

"Sometimes."

"I'll make you a deal," he said. He'd finished his food, and now folded his hands under his chin. "I'll answer any questions you have, if you'll agree to confess one sin to me when we're done."

"Are you serious?"

He nodded.

"We talking venial sins, mortal sins?"

"A sin that means something to you," he said.

I watched him for a moment, then I said, "Were James and Catherine having marital issues?"

"You're a cop?" he said.

"A private investigator."

He dropped his plate into the trash can next to his seat and crossed his arms on the table. "On the day Cat died, they'd been seeing me for marriage counseling for a month."

"I thought you retired?"

He shook his head. "It was nothing official. They didn't pay me or anything like that. I counseled them as a friend."

"What was the problem?"

"Why are you looking into this?" he said.

"I can't say. But I won't do anything to hurt Cat's memory or James' reputation. I'm just following a lead, trying to put a theory to rest."

He looked at me, and I got the sense he believed me, but he was still reserved. "I hate to talk of them this way," he said.

"I handle my investigations with the utmost care," I said. "I won't let slip a word you tell me unless it proves to be crucial in putting away a criminal."

He nodded, thought another moment, and then spoke. "James slept with another woman."

"Who?"

He shrugged. "I didn't ask them that. I don't think Cat even knew. It wasn't relevant."

"How much time passed between the day of the affair and the day they contacted you for counseling?"

"Just a couple of weeks," he said. "James contacted me by phone the day after he confessed it to Catherine. She was beside herself, but they had been having issues for some time. It wasn't a huge shock to her. They both quickly decided they needed mediation." He looked at me. "They loved each other."

"That's what everyone keeps telling me," I said.

"It's true."

I sat there a moment, thinking hard about my next question. Then I asked it: "Could James have played a part in Cat's death?"

"Never." There was no hesitation, nor doubt in his eyes.

"Thank you," I said, getting to my feet. "I think I might go see if there's any of that quiche left."

"What about your confession?" he called after me as I walked toward the reception hall.

"I owe you one," I said.

I found Kimmy standing next to the food table.

"Where's James?" I said.

She shrugged. "He took off a few minutes ago."

"He left?"

"In a hurry," she said. She shook her head slowly, as if lost in thought. "Poor guy. He looked like he was about to break down again. He practically ran out the front door."

I scanned the room for the blonde he'd been talking with near Cat's grave. She was the next person I wanted to talk to. But I didn't see her anywhere. "Did you notice the woman he was talking with earlier?"

"Which one?"

"Young, blond hair," I said.

"Yeah, the one he was fighting with. Who didn't notice? She stomped off right after they spoke. Last time I saw her, she was headed for the parking lot."

It was right then that the gunshot sounded outside. It was muted and nondescript—but I knew the difference between a gunshot and a dropped book, even through several feet of brick, mortar, and steel. I ran out the side door. The park was empty. Father O'Neil was no longer seated at the picnic table. I looked toward the pond and saw the hump of a man's body lying on the slope of grass that angled down gradually toward the water.

The screech of tires.

I turned toward the parking lot and saw a pickup truck whipping gears and racing toward the road. It had a rack hooked up over the truck bed, which was hung with a ladder, rope, and various other construction tools. I tried to get a read on the license plate or the name of the construction company printed on the side of the truck, but it was too far away. All I got was a logo: a blocky, black and white "G," capitalized, and with hard angles.

When the truck was gone I ran toward the pond and took a knee next to the body. I'd known it would be Father O'Neil, but part of me had hoped to find a stranger lying there in the grass.

People had begun to gather around now, and I heard someone scream. A man shouted for someone to call the cops. Kimmy was next to me, and she had her cell phone to her ear.

I felt Father's throat for a pulse, and found one. It was weak, but he was still alive.

"Hang in there," I said, placing my hand on his back.

Kimmy and I stayed with him until the first responders and the EMTs showed up. I gave my statement, which was that I hadn't seen a thing except the logo on the side of the pickup truck. I didn't even know if the driver of the truck was the shooter or a fleeing onlooker. I found out which hospital they were taking him to, so I could visit him later. Then we headed back to Kimmy's place. We didn't speak the whole way there. When we arrived, we sat in my car in the driveway, letting the engine idle.

"You okay?" I said.

"I'm fine," she said.

More quiet.

"Things just got more complicated," I said.

She looked at me, waited for me to explain.

"I got to talk to the priest a little, before he got shot."

"And?"

"And he says he was giving James and Cat marriage counseling. He'd been doing it pro bono for about a month."

"So they *were* having problems."

I nodded, looked at her. "James cheated on her."

She held my gaze a moment, and then her eyes opened up wide. "The blonde at the funeral?"

"That's what I'm wondering," I said.

"You think she did the shooting?"

"Maybe."

"Why would she kill the priest?" she said. "Why go after Chelsea?"

"The priest knew about the affair," I said. "He didn't know who James cheated with, but she doesn't necessarily know that. From the way the priest made it sound, James cut ties with her after one slip. He confessed everything to Cat, and the next day they were in counseling, fighting to save their marriage. Maybe she was upset that Father O'Neil was helping them work things out." I shifted in my seat as Jeffy came out the front door of the house and ran for the car. "As for Chelsea...I don't know."

Jeffy started banging on the window. I rolled it down.

"What's happening?" I said.

"Did you see the dead lady?"

"I did."

"Was she all white and gross like a zombie?"

I shook my head. "No. She looked more like a pretty doll."

He screwed up his face in disgust.

Kimmy opened her door, and the open-door alarm began to ding. "You want to come in for a coffee? Maggie makes Folgers taste gourmet."

"Can't. I've got to head to the office. I'm supposed to meet up with a potential witness. That and Josh says it helps his motivation if I show up occasionally."

"Witness?"

"The old lady I spoke to at the funeral. She lives two houses down from James."

Kimmy stepped out of the car, shut the door and came around to my side. "This was an interesting first date."

"First, but not last?"

Dominic Stabile

She smiled back at me as she led Jeffy toward the house.

Chapter Six

My office was on upper King Street, just a few blocks from Kimmy's bar. It was on the second floor over an empty shop that used to be a vintage clothing store. The main door looked like the front door to a cheap apartment. I'd installed a plate on the door that said, "NICK DIOLI, INVESTIGATIVE SERVICES," but it did little to dispel the sense you were walking into a crack house.

When I entered, Josh quickly dog-eared the book he was reading and started slapping his keyboard, as if he'd been hard at work. Josh was a young guy getting his associate's in Criminal Justice and doing my secretarial work because he had some Hollywood-fed view of my job that almost made me enjoy it again. He was also an amateur bodybuilder, and kept a tangle of resistance bands on and around his office chair. I'd periodically walk in on him engaged in some sort of resistance training, but rarely did I catch him reading a book.

"I take it things have been slow?" I said.

"You haven't gotten a call since I last saw you three days ago."

I nodded. "Remind me what I pay you for."

He began to stammer, coughing up the sort of generic qualifications you might find on the first draft of a sparse resume.

"I'm joking," I said. I took out my wallet and plucked out a twenty, surprised to find it there. "Why don't you run down the street and grab two coffees."

He got up and took the twenty, which probably looked like an oversized gorilla taking a ticket stub from a baby.

"Do you need me to stop by the liquor store?" he said.

"I've still got half a bottle," I said, without looking at him.

On his way out he said, "Oh, there's a lady in your office."

"Better make it three coffees," I said, and he left.

I entered my office and found the old lady from the cemetery sitting in the chair across from my desk.

"My name is Gladys Ester," she said. Her voice wavered. She was nervous, and it made me a little nervous. On top of that, once I started thinking about the bottle in my desk, I couldn't get it out of my mind. My hands were shaking worse now, and I kicked myself for not stopping somewhere for a drink on the way in.

"Nice to me you," I said, taking my seat. "What can I do for you?"

"I saw what happened the night Catherine died," Gladys said.

I took a pad and pencil from my desk, flipped the pad to the first clean page.

"What night was that?" I said.

"You don't know?"

"I need to hear it from you."

"The eighteenth," she said.

I wrote that down. "Do you know around what time?"

"I know the exact time," she said. "It was quarter to eleven. I know because I always have my last cup of tea on the patio at ten thirty."

"Okay. Go ahead."

"I saw Catherine walk out to the pier. Then, not five minutes later, James ran out there. They were both standing on the end of the pier, having a spat. Then Chelsea, the poor girl, ran out there to see what the fuss was. And that's when James, in a fit of rage, shoved Catherine. The railing was loose, it had been for a long time, and I'd written over a dozen letters about it. She hit her head on the edge of the pier and fell into the water. Chelsea went to screaming and ran off."

I finished writing. "Why haven't you spoken to the police about this?"

"I don't want my family involved in any official capacity. It's my moral obligation to make sure the information gets into the right hands, but I'm not interested in making the papers over this."

I nodded. That same sentiment was the reason I'd gotten wrapped up in all this in the first place. It was no surprise.

"How do you know the Tully family?" I said.

"My niece has babysat for them since she was in high school. I've gotten to know them well, especially Chelsea."

"Had you noticed them having any problems?"

She looked down at her lap and thought a moment before speaking. "They'd been fighting a lot before that night," she said. "James has a temper—that was nothing new. But he started drinking a few months ago. Heavily. I spoke to Catherine about it once, about the damage his soul might incur from such behavior. She said he was stressed from work, that he needed the drink to calm his nerves. But all I ever saw was the way it raised his temper, and made his abuses all the bolder."

"He was abusing Cat?"

"Not physically," she said.

I stared down at my pad a moment.

"You're not the first person who's told me James is suspect in all this," I said. "My other source tells me James has been a hot-head all along."

"As long as I've known him," she said. "I used to hear them fighting all the time. I would go out on my patio and see poor Catherine running across the beach. It's probably how her nightly habit started."

"Nightly habit? You mean the night swims?"

She nodded. "The drinking simply made it worse."

"And how did you find out about his drinking?"

"My niece," she said. "She brought it up, and then I noticed all the glass in his recycling."

"You think he'd ever hurt the girl?"

"Chelsea?"

I nodded.

"I don't know," she said. She looked around the room a moment. She had gripped one hand in the other, squeezing her fingers together. She looked at me. "He could. I honestly believe it. I hate to think of it. If he did, I'd have to blame myself. Having witnessed his abusive nature and done nothing to stop it until now. From the things my niece told me, he could certainly put a hand to her with no qualms about it."

"Could he kill her?"

She stared at me. "Are you saying...?"

"Chelsea's alive and well. I'm just curious if you think he's got the stones."

Her eyes widened.

"The *nerve*, is what I mean."

She straightened up in her seat, and a look of chiseled resolve touched her face. "He had the nerve to shove that poor woman into the screaming ocean, so I imagine he'd have the nerve to do the same to Chelsea."

I sat back in my seat and let that settle. Here was eye-witness testimony, a rarity in my business, where I was normally hired to be the eye. I could call Lindsay up now, tell her guess what I had and here's where to send the check. But why would James order a hit on Father O'Neil, even if he was audacious enough to kill Chelsea? And why would he run away just before it happened, eliminating a perfect alibi?

"Are you aware of the shooting that took place today at the funeral?" I said.

The color drained out of her face. "No. I left after I spoke to you."

I nodded. "Father O'Neil was shot today. Would James have a reason to kill him?"

She had placed a hand over her mouth. Her eyes began to shine with tears. She couldn't speak, so she simply shrugged and shook her head, no.

"Do you know who the young blonde was he was arguing with near the grave today?"

She continued to shake her head. After a moment, she swallowed hard, gathered herself. "I only know what I've told you. James shoved Cat off that pier."

I looked at her another moment. If she was lying, she had a better poker face than I did. "Okay," I said.

"So, what are you going to do?" she said.

"The case is ongoing. But I'm going to take your statement into consideration. When the time comes to present things to the proper authorities, you'll be contacted to testify in court that what you've just told me is true. Not too hard, right?"

"I won't testify," Gladys said.

I looked at her. "What?"

"I will not testify."

I put on my patient face, which happens to look just like an impatient person trying to look patient. "Is this a rich people thing?" I said.

She gripped her pocketbook in her lap and looked away from me.

"I don't want a scandal," she said.

"It's a little late for that," I said. "You've just accused a prominent member of society of murdering his own wife. That's as scandalous as we get in this business. I can keep you out of the papers until we know for sure one way or the other, but if you want to talk about moral obligations, you'll need to come forward when it's time to put the pin in him."

"I won't testify," she said again.

I wanted to smack the resolve right off her face—but I don't hit women, I certainly don't hit grandmothers, and, most importantly, I never hit a potential client. "Listen, I'll do what I can without scumming up your family's reputation. But if it comes down to you or nothing, I'll be calling you."

She stood up in a huff, and started toward the door.

Just then a question came to me and I had to ask. "Ms. Ester?"

She stopped and spun around to face me. "What is it?" she said.

"You said it was quarter to eleven when you saw all this go down?"

"Yes."

"Pretty dark on the beach by then, right?"

She blinked a few times, then nodded. "Yes."

"And there aren't any lights out there by the pier, are there?"

"You know there aren't," she said. "But it was a full moon, and I could see clearly enough to know what was going on out there."

I nodded. "Okay, Ms. Ester," I said. "That's all for now." I heard the front door shut and assumed it was Josh back with the coffees.

Josh came around the corner and held out one of the cups to her. But Gladys stormed out, her cane clanking against the floor, and nearly knocked Josh and the three coffees to the floor as she went.

Josh handed me my coffee and went back to his desk. I took the bottle from my desk, free poured a shot into the coffee. I sat there a while trying to figure out what to make of Gladys' story. If what she said was true, James was guilty of manslaughter at most. There was no premeditation. He couldn't have known Cat would die, even if he had shoved her off the pier on purpose. So, if she was telling the truth, why would James be looking to kill his daughter? It was easy to see why Chelsea might have misinterpreted what she saw. Therefore, in either instance, Chelsea's stance made sense. But James didn't have the look of a man who would kill his own daughter just for the just in cases. Maybe if he was staring down a life sentence, but not for manslaughter. And then, again, why kill the priest? Why run out of the reception hall?

I was mulling this over when my cell rang. It was Parker.

"About time," I said. "What do you have?"

"A whole lot of nothing."

"Nothing?"

"James is clean," Parker said. "No criminal history, no ex-wives with axes to grind, no illegitimate children that have come forward. If he's ever done anything seriously wrong, he's done it with no witnesses around."

"That doesn't help at all," I said.

"That's what I have."

I watched the doorway to my office a moment, then said, "I need you to do me another favor."

"Only if you promise to continue letting flow this well-spring of gratitude."

"I need you to check out any construction companies whose logo is the letter G."

"You mean like Grimely?" he said.

"What?"

"Grimely Construction. They're the ones working on the old library lot I was telling you about."

I leaned forward in my seat. "I need you to get me everything you can on them. Every project they're working or have ever worked. Employee names and rap sheets, any and everything you can."

"I've got most of that already," he said. "We've been trying to find something on these guys for weeks."

"Because they're working the library lot?"

"And every other lot BB and T has bought up in the last ten years."

"BB and T?"

"Don't you ever read the paper?" he said. "BB and T is a huge land developer local to Charleston. They've been integral in the push to clean up upper King and St. Phillip Streets. It's a movement that's been gaining speed for the last ten years."

"So they're the reason the rent on my office just went up," I said.

"Yours and everyone else who likes living or running a business on the peninsula."

I sat there a moment, deciding what I wanted to do first. I suddenly had a lot of work ahead of me.

"Is that all?" Parker said.

"Get me everything you have on Grimely and BB and T. I'll meet you at Kimmy's in an hour."

He started to say something, but I hung up on him.

I drove out to Roper Hospital to check up on Father O'Neil. He'd been moved from the emergency ward into intensive care, where they'd finally managed to stabilize him. From what I was told by the attending nurse, the bullet had missed his heart by a quarter of an inch; but it was still in there, and he was awaiting surgery. I'd reserved the hope I might be able to ask him if he saw his shooter, but he was sleeping under the power of a great deal of drugs.

When I entered his room, the man seated next to Father O'Neil's bed practically jumped to his feet.

James.

He looked at me a moment, his eyes wide with expectation. Those eyes were raw, too, like he'd been crying. I thought, for just a second, that he was going to run. Then he slumped back into his seat and turned his eyes back to the Father.

I stood there another moment, then entered the room and shut the door behind me.

Whiskey for Breakfast

I sat in a chair on the opposite side of the bed from where James sat. I watched James a minute, waiting to see if he would say something, then I said, "You want to tell me what's going on?"

"It's none of your business," he said. He'd taken Father O'Neil's hand. He watched the man's face, as if he expected him to begin speaking any moment.

"Do you know who did this?"

James shook his head. "This isn't the time or the place for this conversation."

"What are you hiding? What secret is so important you'll let people die for it? People you obviously care about."

"You have no clue what you're talking about," he said.

"Why don't you set me straight then?" I said. "I've got half a dozen people, including your daughter, who seem to think you're a cold-blooded murderer."

That got his attention. He looked up at me now, his eyes gone wide. "You said you couldn't find her."

"I found her," I said. "Or rather, she found me. Grandma and the gang nearly knocked my head off. Tied me up, screened me, and then sent me back here to find out the truth about Cat's death."

"You know the truth," he said, looking away.

I watched his face, thought long and hard before I spoke again. "Do you even know that someone tried to kill Chelsea?"

He looked up at me again, and I knew instantly that this was the first he'd heard of it. "What are you talking about?" he said.

"All I know is someone broke into the bakery with a knife and a mask over his face." I left out the part about Virginia shooting the intruder.

James got to his feet and began to pace the room. "But she was okay?"

"When I last saw her she was."

He nodded and continued to pace.

"The person who wants Chelsea dead," I said. I nodded toward Father O'Neil. "Could that be the same person who put a bullet in our friend here?"

"I don't know," he said, and it was the first thing I'd heard him say since I walked in that had the ring of truth to it.

"You know something," I said. "And you need to start talking."

"There's nothing for me to say. I don't know who would want to hurt Chelsea or Father O'Neil, and I have no idea how the two things could be connected."

I stared at him, and I felt my patience boiling off of me in heat waves. "Why'd you run out of the reception hall today?"

"What?"

"You ran out of the reception hall less than ten minutes before the shooting. I'd call that a suspicious coincidence."

"I couldn't take it anymore," he said. "All of those people I never speak to, telling me how sorry they are." He looked at me, and I saw real anger in his eyes. "I could hear them gossiping, speculating. I know people think I did it. I'm not an idiot."

I gave that candid outburst a moment to dissipate, then I said, "Who was the blonde you were arguing with at the funeral?"

He shook his head and reached out for the arm of his chair. He steadied himself and then sat down. "I just want all of this to go away," he said.

"You need to talk to me," I said. "I'm here to make sure Chelsea gets through this alive."

"What do you care?" he said. "I mailed out your check this afternoon."

"I'm off your payroll," I said. "I've been hired to find out the truth about Cat's death. Yesterday, I thought it was a safe bet you'd killed her and now you were after Chelsea to keep her quiet."

"That's ridiculous," he said.

"I'm beginning to see that. But I still have a job to do. *Someone* went after Chelsea, and *your* watch was stuck in the boards of the pier with the broken railing. One way or the other, Cat went over the pier, and Chelsea saw it happen. One way or the other, *you* were cheating on Cat with another woman, and I think she was the cute blonde at the funeral today. I think *she* might have good reason to want Father O'Neil dead, but I don't see why she'd want to kill Chelsea. I can't put it all together, but one thing I don't buy for a second is that all of this death and murder and attempted murder is happening all around you by coincidence."

He wouldn't look at me.

I sat there a minute and then said, "I think it's time to involve the police in this."

His eyes widened and he got to his feet. "No. We can't."

"It's *we* now?"

He came around the bed and stood in front of me, his hands out as if to grip the tail of my coat in pleading. Thankfully, he didn't. "Please. No cops. I'll tell you what I *do* know if you promise not to involve the police."

"What is it with you people?"

"It's the affair," he said, pacing around the bed and sitting down in his seat again. He rested his elbows on his knees and stared at the floor awhile. "I don't want the affair in the papers."

"Why would the affair have to come out? I'm talking about whoever is trying to kill Chelsea. Whoever shot Father O'Neil. Unless you're admitting it's the blonde doing the killing."

"I don't know who went after Chelsea," he said. "I don't know who shot Father O'Neil. But I want him caught as badly as you do. More so, in fact."

"What do you know?"

"I know that I didn't kill Cat. But you're right: she went off the pier."

I waited for him to explain.

He swallowed hard. "Cat knew about the affair by then. I'd confessed it to her, and we'd begun to see Father O'Neil for counseling. I'd cut all ties with the woman I'd cheated with, and I'd told her never to contact me again. But she did. Cat and I were doing better. We were getting past this mess and our lives were just returning to normal when the phone rang on the night of the eighteenth and Cat answered."

"It was the blonde," I said.

He nodded. "She demanded to speak to me. When Cat refused her, she began to tell my wife all of these horrible things."

"What sorts of things?"

His face flushed. "The things we'd done. You know...together."

"Got it."

"I took the phone from Cat and blessed the girl out and hung up on her. I went to Cat, tried to comfort her, but everything we'd gained from our counseling had been lost. That was how it suddenly seemed. I remembered the way I'd felt with the other woman, and Cat's fears—the things she'd imagined we'd done—had been confirmed. Cat ran out onto the pier that night. I went after her, still trying to make my case, hopelessly."

"You were fighting," I said, trying to speed things along. "You got worked up, gave her a shove, and she went over."

"No," he said.

"She didn't jump," I said.

"No," he said.

"Then what?"

He looked at me. "She slipped."

"You mean she slipped and said the wrong thing, so you hit her before you knew what was happening?"

"No," he said. "I mean that the railing gave beneath her, she slipped, hit her head, and went into the water."

I laughed. Not because death is funny. It's not. I didn't find any humor in the image of Cat going over that pier into the dark ocean. I laughed because it was so obvious to me James was putting me on, that it seemed the only appropriate response.

He only looked at me, an expression of mild shock on his face.

"You're serious?" I said.

"Chelsea was watching from the beach. When I reached for Cat to catch her before she went in, I guess it looked like I was shoving her over the edge." He showed me his wrist, and I saw the three scratch marks there again. "My watch snapped, and I lost my grip on her. If I hadn't grabbed her hand she probably wouldn't have hit her head." He was looking at the floor, thinking aloud now.

I didn't say anything else for a while, trying to swallow this story.

"Did you go in after her?" I said.

"Of course. I looked for hours. But it was dark and the tide was in. I couldn't find her."

"So what then?" I said. "That story ain't in the papers."

"I had to think," he said, holding his hands out toward me again, as if begging for my understanding the way a panhandler might beg for change. "I went inside the house, and Chelsea was gone. But I couldn't think of that. Not then. I *had* to figure out a different story. She was already dead."

"So you cooked up the part about the little tiff, and her going for her usual night swim and never coming back."

He nodded, dropping his face into his open hand. "I got rid of my wet clothes and waited until morning to report her missing."

"Why didn't you just come clean with the cops?"

He shook his head, and it took him a moment to get his bearings. "If I'd told them the truth, they'd have pried."

"My understanding is that you've got pull with cops."

"To an extent," he said. "But they would have launched an investigation, if for no other reason, so that they could say they'd ruled out murder. They would have checked my phone

75

records, interviewed my neighbors. I couldn't risk them finding out about the affair."

I looked at him a moment. "So this wasn't even about escaping a possible murder charge. You just didn't want bad press."

He nodded, but he wouldn't look at me.

I had a lot of things I wanted to say to that. But, instead, I exhaled a long breath, and watched my lap a moment. When I spoke again my voice was even and mostly free of disdain. "I want to speak with the blonde."

He shook his head. "No."

"I'll need a name and a number. An address would be good, too."

"No," he said again. He still wouldn't look at me.

"No?"

"Leave her out of it," he said. "It's not her."

"All the same, I'd like to see what she knows."

He looked at me. "She doesn't know a thing. Do you want to know why she was at the funeral? She was upset with me because I haven't called her since Cat's death."

"She sounds unbalanced," I said.

He nodded. "But not a murderer."

My cell phone vibrated. I took it from my pocket. It was a text from Parker: "Where are you?"

I stood, tucking the phone back into my jacket. "We're not done," I said. "I need you to stay in town and be available."

He nodded, but had turned his eyes back to the priest. "There's one more thing," he said.

"What's that?" I said.

"The real reason I ran out of the reception hall today." He dug in his pocket and removed a folded slip of paper. "A man approached me I didn't recognize. Tall, built like a house. He shook my hand, and slipped me this message. I ran out to find him, to demand an explanation. But he was gone."

Whiskey for Breakfast

I took the paper and opened it. There was a short, typewritten sentence: KEEP YOUR MOUTH SHUT, OR THIS IS YOU.

Chapter Seven

It was after seven, and Kimmy's was unusually crowded. Even my spot at the end of the bar was taken. Kimmy had her hands full with customers. She was good under pressure, and she knew how to work a tip out of someone; but right now she look frazzled. I figured I'd wait until things died down before I bothered her.

I saw Parker in a booth along the back wall with a laptop open on the table, and I slipped in across from him. He was sipping on some local microbrew I didn't recognize, and staring intently at his computer screen. It took a second before I realized he was unaware of my presence. I slapped the table and he nearly spilled his beer on the keyboard.

"That's twice in one day," I said.

He said something in reply, but I couldn't hear him over the noise of the room.

"What?"

He gave me a frustrated look and spun his laptop around to face me. Then he came over to my side and slipped into the booth next to me.

"Are we one of those same-side-of-the-booth couples?" I said.

He stared at me a second, shaking his head slightly in disbelief. "You know, I don't do this for pleasure," he said.

"It's a tough economy," I said. "A girl should do what a girl's gotta do. I simply won't be a part of it."

His expression didn't change, but his head stopped shaking. "I'm talking about feeding you information. This isn't fun for me. I'm not just off my last high, looking to crack a few jokes before my next dose. I work three jobs and run this paper, basically by myself. I'm also a full-time student."

For once, I removed the shit-eating grin from my face. "Why do you help me, then?"

He shrugged and looked away. "At the odd chance you might do some good," he said.

I nodded, and decided I'd stop picking on him for now. "What do you have?"

He pointed at the *Post and Courier* article currently up on the screen. I skimmed the article. There was an unflattering head shot of a bloated man with a weak mustache, balding head, and a look in his bespectacled eyes that told me he was used to overhearing the things people said about him in public places. Roald Ester.

I looked up at Parker. "Any relation to a Gladys Ester?"

He pointed toward the caption beneath Roald's photo, which made mention of his wife, Gladys, and live-in niece, Jessica.

I noted this and continued to read the article. Roald had studied architecture at Cornell, but quickly fell into real estate and land development. He was currently the Head of BB&T, and the brains behind the city's push to "class up" the "seedier" corners of downtown Charleston: namely upper King and St. Philip Streets. Residents in the area had been migrating north for years now, as the cost of living climbed. He was responsible for the turnover of nearly a dozen condemned buildings and low-rent apartments, putting up two hotels, three chain restaurants, and a slew of condo-style apartments with a monthly rent meant to keep out the trash, all in the last ten years. Apparently he had a huge overhaul planned for upper King. A whole string of affordable housing units was set to be demolished so they could continue King Street's shopping district on past Spring Street. This was just waiting approval from the city council.

Parker summarized another article, this one from the *Charleston City Paper*, which talked of the comments Roald had made in favor of setting a midnight curfew for bars, which would effectively eradicate the Charleston nightlife. I didn't have much stock in the Charleston nightlife, to be honest, but I knew there was a chance it would hurt Kimmy's business. God knew she was struggling as it was. Though today was no indication of that.

As Parker summarized several other articles, I grew to know one thing for sure: there were a lot of people out there who would love to see Roald get smeared. No wonder Gladys was being so careful. What I didn't understand was what any of this had to do with James Tully.

"What about Grimely Construction?" I said. "I've got a theory one of their employees may have been involved in the shooting of a priest."

He didn't miss a beat. "Grimely is a small, family owned company. The guy who started it, Drayton Grimely, has somehow managed to get on Roald's payroll for all of his foreseeable reconstruction projects in Charleston. It's kind of odd, as Grimely is neither the biggest nor the best construction company in Charleston. They do a little of everything, and they've taken big jobs in the past, but again, they're small potatoes."

"Any ex-cons on Grimely's payroll?"

"No less than five," Parker said. "Five that I could dig up."

"Equal opportunity employer," I said.

Parker nodded. "One of them, Max Henderson, quit Grimely last year. Another, Reed Houser, got seven years for armed robbery in 2009. That leaves three still employed: John Clayton, Michael Williams, and Marcus White."

"What are their demons?"

Parker closed out the screen he was on and pulled up another. I saw the mug shots of each guy he'd just named. He dropped out all but the last three. "Marcus was snagged for possession of marijuana—nothing huge. But John and Michael have both been away more than once for assault, armed robbery, resisting arrest, DUI—the list goes on." He looked at me. "They read more like career criminals."

"I know the type," I said, taking a moment to memorize their features. "Do you have addresses for these guys?"

He reached into his computer bag and removed a manila folder. "I've got everything we just went over printed. You've got the mug shots, addresses, phone numbers, and rap sheets."

I was impressed, and I kicked myself that he saw it on my face.

"I know," he said, closing his laptop and tucking it away. He got to his feet, zipped up his computer bag and slung it over his shoulder. "I won't bother asking for compensation. Just have a drink for me, okay? That's something I know you'll actually do."

He walked away just as Kimmy was coming over with a bottle of Johnny Walker and a glass. "You didn't even say hello," she said, pouring two fingers of scotch into the glass and setting it on my table.

"You looked busy," I said.

"I am," she said. Someone called her from across the room. She held up an index finger and turned back to me. She raised her eyebrows. "At this rate I'll have no problem putting Jeffy through college."

I smiled and she hurried away toward the man who'd called for her. I picked up my glass, said, "Here's to you, Parker," and drank.

Chapter Eight

It was getting late in the evening, and all of downtown was cast in that ember-orange haze that turns every color it touches to ash. I'd decided I would swing by the liquor store and then head home. I would read over the files Parker had given me and plan out my next move. I saw breaking and entering in my future, and figured I should get a few hours' sleep before I started cracking windows.

I was halfway down the block when my cell rang. It was Josh.

"You still at the office?"

"We're open until 7:00," he said.

"Really?"

"There's a woman here who needs to talk with you."

"Story of my life," I said. "Who?"

"Says her name is Lindsay. She's got a badge."

"I'll be right there."

Lady Cop was seated before my desk with her legs crossed. She wore black boots, blue jeans, and a thin, white t-shirt. She looked up at me when I walked in, a touch of amusement in her eyes.

"So this is the lair?" she said.

I smiled to let her know I was invincible. I sat in my chair, leaned back and kept that smile as I looked at her a moment. "You drove a long way just to make fun of my office," I said.

She kept her smile, too, making a show of scanning the room. "I have to ask, do you get a lot of damsels in distress knocking on your door just before closing time?"

"I assume you're here for a status update?" My smile faltered and I went ahead and got rid of it. "Funny thing is I thought I gave you my card."

"You did," she said, dropping her smile. "That's how I found your office." She stood and placed her hands on the back of the chair. When she spoke next there was no amusement in her voice. "What do you have on James?"

"Only that he's innocent," I said. I took the bottle and two glasses from the desk. I filled the glasses and slid one toward her, then sipped at mine. I did all of this before looking up to see her reaction. Her expression told me she wasn't sure whether or not I was joking.

"How do you know that?"

"A lot's happened since I got back to Charleston," I said. I gave her the rundown, telling her about the watch and the broken railing on the pier; I told her about the shooting at the funeral, the affair, and James' tearful explanation of Cat's accidental death. I told her about the note James had shown me at the hospital and my lead on the ex-cons working for Grimely. By the time I finished catching her up, she'd sat down and gone through two glasses of whiskey.

She was quiet for a moment, rearranging things in her mind. And I understood how she felt. You get so fixed on the idea that this or that guy is the perp, you begin to associate your future peace with his downfall. Bringing him in becomes your life's aim. When you're forced to accept you've been chasing the wrong guy, it takes some time to adjust. Personally, I thought she was taking it well.

"So what's your angle?" she said. "How does Grimely connect with James?"

"That's the part I can't figure out," I said. "All I know is that the shooter was likely the person driving that Grimely truck. I'm fairly certain James is telling the truth about Cat, which means someone else sent that man after Chelsea, and someone else shot Father O'Neil."

"Who would want Chelsea and the priest dead?"

"My current theory—whoever has the most to lose if news of James' affair gets out."

"You think Chelsea knows about the affair?"

"I think it's highly likely. She was in the house when Cat and James fought."

We were both quiet, moving the evidence around, trying to figure out where the pieces fit.

"It's either James or the woman he cheated with," Lindsay said.

"I suspect the woman is involved, but I couldn't get James to give her up. And that still doesn't explain Grimely or the man who handed the threatening letter to James."

"So, what's next?" she said.

I looked at her. "Next we find out why you're really here."

She adjusted in her seat. "I came here to make sure you were doing everything you could to bring Cat's killer to justice."

I shook my head. "I don't believe that. You could have found out everything I just told you with a phone call."

She was quiet.

"Well?"

Her eyes lit up in a way I didn't like. "Okay," she said. "You're right. It's not all about making sure you're doing your job right—though that's a big part of it."

I put up a hand to stop her. "For the record, murder investigation is not my job."

"It's the job I hired you for," she said. "The other reason I'm here is the dead body we found in the ravine. The one I told you about last time we spoke."

"Yeah? What about him?" I said. I'm fairly good at playing dumb.

"Firstly, I never said it was a man," she said. "Secondly, he's from Charleston."

Not dumb enough. I nodded, trying to maintain a neutral expression. "I meant 'him' in the gender neutral sense. You think the DOA is connected to this case?"

She smiled and leaned back in her seat. With the self-assured expression she wore now, an outside observer would have assumed this was her office. "You trying to say this is the first time that crossed your mind?"

"You mentioned the dead person in passing. I had no reason to give it a second thought until just now."

Her smile hardened, and she narrowed her eyes. For the second time since we'd met, I felt like she'd walked me into a trap and had me spring it on myself. "You can say 'him'," she said. "The dead person is a *him*."

"Okay."

She kept looking at me.

I leaned my elbows on the desk and tried to look unmoved. "Why don't you just say what you came here to say?"

She stared at me another moment, then said, "Does the name Michael Williams mean anything to you?"

"The body from the ravine is Michael Williams?"

She nodded.

I looked at her for a long time, mentally debating the wisdom of my next move. Then I took the manila folder from my lap and slapped it on the desk. I opened it and flipped through to the mug shots Parker had printed up for me. I placed my finger on the image of Michael Williams. "He's in my top three," I said.

She stared at the picture, and something changed in her face. The idea that we were getting close seemed to trump her suspicion of me, at least for the moment. "Shit," she said.

"That's what I'm thinking," I said.

She looked up at me, and that suspicion was back. "I know you know something about Michael's death."

I put up my hands in surrender. "This coincidence shocks me as much as it shocks you."

"So, I suppose it would shock you if I said Michael was shot?"

I kept my eyes even with hers. "Guys like Michael always go bloody," I said.

"Uh-huh. So, what's next?"

"First, I want to show James these mug shots, see if he recognizes any of these guys as the man from the funeral who slipped him the note. Obviously, I can cross Michael off the list."

"And if that turns up nothing?"

My smile came back. "A little B and E?"

She left to meet with a Detective Cohen of City PD to go over what she knew of Michael Williams' death. Because Michael was a Charleston native, she was hoping to consult with Cohen to get to the bottom of his murder. But she didn't leave before assuring me we still had some things to discuss. I'll be honest: I wasn't looking forward to that discussion.

But I was glad to get rid of her for the moment. I'd told her the whole B and E thing was a joke; but, it wasn't, and I got the feeling she knew that. I also got the feeling she hoped to join me for the duration of my investigation, and I wasn't happy about that either. I'd have trouble doing things the way I found best to do them with her around.

My plan was to stake out John Clayton's house first. Considering that Marcus White's only recorded offense was a possession charge and Michael was dead, I had a good feeling about John's place. I'd wait until he left and sneak in, see what I could turn up. I didn't know what I was looking for, but I didn't know what else to do. After Lindsay had left my office, I'd called James several times, getting his answering machine.

I didn't know where he was and I didn't have his cell number, so I decided to be proactive.

John had a small house in North Charleston. His neighborhood was at the end of a long frontage road that skirted the interstate. The houses were old, pre Hurricane Hugo. You could see how some of them sat uncertainly on their foundations. I'd grown up in a pre-Hugo house, and I still remember how, years after Hugo had struck, I'd hear the sound of wind humming through the invisible gap of space between the floor and wall at the head of my bed at night.

There was a gravel lot that ran between two houses a little ways down from his place, and I pulled in there and popped my hood. It was dark out now, and humid. The crickets and cicadas were making their noise. I leaned under the hood, as if I were tinkering with the engine, and, occasionally, I peeked up to see the situation at his place. I knew it wasn't a foolproof plan. It was late, and chances were good that he was in for the night. But, again, I had nothing else to do until I could get in touch with James, and this might be my last chance at doing things my way without Lindsay's interference.

The first thing I noticed was there was no car in his driveway. I knew from Parker's reports that John was single. There would likely only be one car, and it could be in the garage. But there were no lights on in the house. I pulled my cell and checked the time: 8:30. Construction was a hard job, but 8:30 just seemed like an early bedtime for a restless criminal like Mr. Clayton. I had the feeling he wasn't the teeth-brushed-and-tucked-in-bed-by-8:30 type. That meant he probably wasn't home, and probably was good enough for me to take a closer look.

I quietly closed the hood of my car and started toward his house. I figured I'd knock first, make it look good with any nosy neighbors, and I'd know for sure if he was home.

"Car trouble?"

I'd just reached the sidewalk at the base of his lawn when I heard the voice. I was standing under an orange streetlamp.

Whiskey for Breakfast

Moths ticked away at the lamp during the quiet pause before I saw the figure crossing the street. For a second he was just a vague shadow. Then he reached the circle of light set down by the streetlamp, and I saw it was John Clayton. He was tall, broad-shouldered. His head was bald, but it looked intentional, and it complemented his squared jaw and blocky features. He was walking a small, black and white terrier and smoking a cigarette.

"Only when I drive it," I said, but he'd caught me by surprise, and I got the feeling too much of that surprise came through in my voice.

"Didn't mean to scare you," he said. He stopped next to me on the sidewalk. His dog had taken an attack stance, and was letting out a low, steady growl. "Quiet, Checkers," he said.

I smiled, trying to disguise my apprehension while I thought about whether or not I wanted to abort altogether. "Checkers?"

He nodded. "You know, black and white."

"I thought it was red and black," I said.

He shrugged, unmoved. "I didn't name him." He crouched down and petted the dog a moment. Then he looked up at me. "What brings you to the neighborhood?"

I shrugged, and had no idea what I was going to say until the words began to stumble over my lips. "I used to live in this neighborhood," I said. "Sometimes I just like to drive through, reminisce."

He kept his eyes on me as he ruffled the dog's fur. His cigarette sat pinched in one corner of his mouth. "They say he who lives in the past is already dead." He stood, took the cigarette from his mouth and exhaled smoke. His eyes still didn't leave me. It was then I noticed the tail of his t-shirt over his right hip, the way it bowed out a little more than the left side. It was the way it looked when someone had a gun stuffed in his pants.

I nodded, but, for once, had nothing to say.

He watched me another moment, then laughed. "I'm messing with you," he said, and his right hand slipped down and brushed over the hump on his right hip, briefly, as if he was making sure it was within reach. "How can I help?"

"I could use your phone," I said, deciding I'd get inside one way or the other. I couldn't snoop around the way I'd planned. But I could get a general lay of the land, see if anything stood out. I didn't care that he was packing. So was I, and I bet I was a better shot.

He watched me a second. "No cell phone?"

I shook my head. "Battery died."

He smiled, reached into his pocket, took out a cell phone of his own and handed it to me.

I tried to hold a neutral expression as I took it from him. I swiped my finger over the screen to unlock it and dialed Kimmy. I guessed I was playing out the broken down car act for the Oscar.

"So you think he knows you?" Kimmy said. She'd dropped Jeffy off at Maggie's and come to pick me up. I'd sat with my car for half an hour waiting on her, and John hadn't invited me in. He'd stood with me next to my car, making small talk, as if he wanted to keep me in sight.

"I don't think he knows me," I said. "I just think he's careful. He wasn't letting me inside for anything."

"Why didn't you ask for a glass of water or something?" she said.

I shook my head. "I think I was too off my game by then. I just needed to get out before he saw right through me."

"But you think he's the shooter?"

"It's possible," I said. "It would help if I could get in touch with James." I told her about the mug shots.

"Why don't you just drive out there?" she said. "Maybe he's just not answering his phone right now. He must be getting a hundred calls a day from friends and relatives, paying their respects."

"I don't envy him that," I said.

"So, what's next?"

"Next, I go home and get some sleep."

"What are you going to do about your car?"

I looked at her. "You think you can give me a ride back out there tomorrow. I figure I'll pick it up while he's at work."

She shook her head, but there was a smile. "Remind me why I hang out with you."

Chapter Nine

The next morning, Kimmy drove me out to John Clayton's neighborhood and dropped me off with my car; and I did what I'd intended to do the night before.

I pulled my car deeper into the gravel lot. The lot ended in a cul-de-sac that cut into a dense wood. I parked there, out of view of the street, and moved along the privacy fence surrounding John Clayton's backyard. I went around front and tried the doorbell, like I'd meant to do last night. I did this, again, to disarm nosy neighbors, and to be sure Clayton wasn't home. If he was, I could always make some excuse for dropping by, though I had no plan for what that excuse might be, and it would certainly be an awkward interaction I hoped I didn't have to endure.

I tried the bell three times, giving it about fifteen seconds between each ring.

He wasn't home.

Next I went around back, and moved along the fence toward the woods. It was edging up on 8:00 am, and the sun was just peeking over the pines that cut a jagged line in the sky at the back of the neighborhood. It was warm, and the air was moist. When I reached the end of the fence I cut right, moved along the back fence for a few feet, looked around, and then hopped it.

His backyard was mostly hard-packed dirt with a few islands of thin, scorched grass. I crossed to the patio and tried the sliding glass door. It was locked. I went to the large kitchen window and tried it, keeping my eye on the adjacent neighbor's yard. The window was locked. There was a smaller window on the other side of the door. It was higher up, and almost too narrow, but I inspected it anyway, and found that it was open. Sunlight hitting the screen had hid this fact, but up close I could feel the cool breeze of an air-conditioner, and I could hear a toilet running.

I looked around again to make sure I wasn't being watched, and then I took a pocketknife from my pants pocket, pried it open, and cut out the screen.

It was a chore, but I managed to haul myself through the tiny opening. I worried, at one point, I'd get stuck and John would show up this afternoon with a twitching drunk snagged in his bathroom window; but I finally slid through and fell to the floor. I hit the linoleum on my shoulders, my feet landing in the sink. For a second, I just laid there thinking. Really *thinking*. Then I picked myself up and passed into the adjoining bedroom.

The guy was neat. King sized bed, tightly made; vacuum tracks in the 1970s brown carpet. One thing about bad guys, the good ones got so used to cleaning up after themselves, the habit bled into most aspects of their lives. Even down to the way they kept house. When they got that good, it usually meant they'd been in the business awhile.

I didn't want to spend too much time here, so I gave the room a cursory glance, looking for anything that stood out. Then I went out into the hallway and made for the front of the house. The house was dark, and there was a smell of pasta and old coffee as I drew closer to the kitchen. There was a table just off the hallway covered in mail, some opened and some not. I wasn't surprised to find a heap of bills. It looked like he'd opened a few, and then after a while he'd stopped looking: SCE&G, Southeast Bank, Verizon: he owed everybody money. Once I'd finished with the mail, I proceeded to search the place from wall to wall.

To an outside observer, I would have looked like a mental case, checking the backs of hanging picture frames, beneath coasters, inside the disk slot of his DVD player. But, as a drunk, I knew how to hide things. I'd once filled a new garden hose with vodka, and left it coiled in the yard. I'd tell my wife I was going out to do yard work, and I'd bring a glass of lemonade with me. When you really got down to it, you just never knew. I checked everywhere, looking for anything. What did I hope to find? A letter from Roald Ester or Gladys or James or somebody ordering the hit on Father O'Neil or Chelsea. At this point, I'd have taken the whole case in a take-out container with free egg rolls for my wait, and thank you very much.

But that wasn't to be.

Once I realized I wasn't going to find anything, I went out the way I'd come in, which was a little easier this time. I got in my car and headed for James' house.

He answered after the fourth time I rang the bell, looking worse for wear. He wore a bath robe, and a mask of stubble from the base of his neck up to his eyes. He smelled flammable.

"What is it?" he said.

I pushed my way inside and went for his bar. I poured myself a glass of gin and took a seat on his couch, setting the manila folder on the cushion next to me. He stood at the door watching me a moment, then he shut the door and made himself a drink. He sat on the sofa opposite me and waited dimly for me to speak.

"I've been calling you," I said.

He looked into his glass. "I've been busy."

"I can see that."

He looked at me briefly, took a sip of his drink, and then kept his eyes in his glass as he said, "Why are you here?"

I smiled. "What do you know about Grimely Construction?"

He shrugged and sipped his drink. "Not a single thing," he said.

"What about Roald Ester?"

He paused on that name, then smoothed out the tail of the robe over his leg, trying to look casual. "He's a neighbor of mine," he said. He shrugged. "I've spoken to him once or twice."

"Really?"

He nodded.

"Roald's wife, Gladys, tells me their niece has been baby-sitting for you for years," I said, and I watched his eyes open up, and some vitality flow down through his limbs. That was fear.

"Well, yes, that's true," he said.

"She says you and Chelsea and Cat were close friends of theirs."

He dropped his shoulders slowly, and the corners of his eyes seemed to arch down as his face went limp. "What's your point?"

"Roald runs BB and T, which currently holds a series of contracts with Grimely Construction."

He shrugged. "Okay."

"I'm pretty certain a Grimely employee shot Father O'Neil, and another went after Chelsea."

He looked at me, resting his elbows on his knees. His half-full glass hung between his legs. "Any idea which employees?"

I got up and walked across the room. I opened the folder to the mug shots and dropped it on his lap. He held his drink out to one side and looked down at the photos. He stared for a little too long, and I got nervous that the case was about to hit a wall. But then he dropped his finger heavily on the photo of John Clayton.

"That him?" I said.

He nodded and looked up at me. "He's the one who handed me the note."

I shot the rest of my drink and set the glass on the coffee table. "Why would someone at Grimely want to cover up your affair?"

His mouth tightened. "What?"

I sat next to him on the arm of the sofa. "What I'm figuring is someone's going after everyone who knows about the affair."

"I don't understand."

I pointed at the photo of Michael Williams. "Michael goes after Chelsea and John Clayton goes after Father O'Neil. They both knew about the affair, right?"

He looked down at his hands, his head shaking slightly from side to side. "We tried to keep it from Chelsea, but she overheard us arguing. And we were seeing Father O'Neil for counseling about it." He looked at me. "I don't know why anyone at Grimely would want to cover it up. I wanted it covered up, but I wouldn't have killed for it. I don't know anyone who works for Grimely. I never met John Clayton before in my life until the funeral."

I nodded and went back to the bar to make myself another drink. I filled the glass and shot it before pouring another and taking my seat on the arm of the sofa. I sipped this glass and thought a moment. "But you *do* know someone who works for BB and T."

He nodded, his eyes cast away from me. "I know Roald. But we're old friends." He looked at me, and I saw something in his eyes. Realization. Dawning, unwelcome realization. But he quickly looked away and stammered, "He'd have no m-motive."

"Now see, that's not convincing, James." I sipped my drink and stood. "What aren't you telling me?"

He looked like he was on the verge of a stroke when the doorbell rang. He let out a harsh breath of relief, as if he'd just broken the surface of water after a deep plunge. He got to his feet and moved toward the door faster than I would have thought him capable in his current condition.

He opened the door a crack, and leaned out. He made a noise that sounded like the beginning of a cry for help.

There were three gunshots.

I'd pulled my gun and taken my first step toward the door before I realized I'd dropped my glass.

I saw James slide down to his knees and fall against the door, pressing it shut. I gripped him under his arms and slid him away from the door. I laid him out on his back and checked for a pulse. Nothing. His robe hung open, and I saw the three heavy-caliber wounds focused close together just to the left of his sternum.

By the time I'd pulled the front door open and moved out into the light, I could already hear the roar of an engine. A red pickup was spinning tires on the road out front. It wasn't a Grimely truck this time, but I could see it was John Clayton in the driver's seat. I ran toward him with my gun raised, but he peeled away before I got to him, and I didn't want to shoot and risk hitting one of the neighboring houses.

I went for my car, but he'd slashed my tires.

I called the cops and waited on James' sofa, sipping at a fresh glass. Lindsay and Detective Cohen showed up shortly after the first responder and the EMTs.

"You okay?" Lindsay said. She wore jeans and a white blouse with the sleeves rolled up. Her badge was exposed on her waist, and her holster was clipped to her belt on the opposite hip. She looked like a cop from a movie. One that plays by her own rules—dress code be damned. I sat there, ignoring her question and trying to think of a way to make fun of her about that.

A tall, broad-shouldered black man stood next to her who I knew to be Detective Cohen; I'd met him once, just long enough to turn over a stolen car case that became a homicide after I opened the trunk to find a body that looked the way you might expect a dead body to look if it had been sitting in a trunk for a couple weeks. Cohen was more formally dressed than Lindsay: blue button down tucked into black slacks; tan coat over a shoulder holster. His shoes had a shine to them. He could have been the manager of a Kinko's on his way to an annual meeting, if not for the badge winking at me from his belt.

"Looks fine to me," Cohen said, eying me with just about the right amount of suspicion. I'd been a cop most of my life, but I rarely got along with cops these days. To his credit, I *was* drunk, sitting on a dead man's couch with the dead man lying on the floor in his own blood not ten feet away.

I set my glass on the end table and brushed my hands over my jacket. "I've got a story to tell."

Cohen swept his eyes over the floor until they landed on James' body near the door. "I bet it's a good one."

Lindsay stepped forward and sat on the couch next to me. "What happened here?"

It wasn't until that moment that I realized I had James' blood on my hands, literally. I instinctively wiped them on my lap, but the blood had mostly dried.

I looked at Lindsay. "Anything on Michael Williams?"

She nodded toward Cohen. "City's had a case open on Michael for over a year," she said. She looked at me like she wanted to hold back, then she let it spill. "Michael has had a little side business going with his friend, John Clayton. Theft, murder, either/or on a contract basis for the past few years."

"Hired guns?" I said.

"Old west style," she said.

I thought about that a moment. I thought about where I stood with this case. My instinct was to hold back what I knew, but I typically had a client to protect, and a paycheck to procure. That's when it hit me: after all I'd been through with this case, I likely wasn't getting paid. With nothing to lose, I told them what I knew.

"John Clayton did this," I said.

Lindsay and Cohen glanced at each other.

"You're sure?" Cohen said. He was looking at my hands.

I nodded and kept my eyes on the coffee table. "I came over to show James some photos, see if he could pick out the guy who'd threatened him at the funeral. He pointed out John Clayton."

"Wait, so Clayton is the one who handed James the note?" Lindsay said.

"He shot Father O'Neil, too."

"How do you know that?" Lindsay said.

"John and Michael both work for Grimely Construction. The shooter at the funeral drove a Grimely truck."

Cohen let go a doubtful laugh. "That's your only connection?"

I looked at him. "Got a better one? I just said James identified Clayton. I saw the man myself before he took off today."

His smile disappeared. "I've got a dead man on the floor, little more than six feet from your red hands. I'm not sure your word is good currency at the moment."

I laughed. "That's brilliant. So I did it? I suppose I slashed my own tires, too?"

"I never said you were completely stupid," Cohen said.

I looked at Lindsay. "Help me out here."

She shrugged. "I can't do anything about the way this looks," she said.

"I called you," I said, looking back and forth between the two of them. "You hired me to look into James."

She looked uncertain. She wanted to believe me, but she was bogged down in the facts she could prove. "The first time I met you, you were coming for Chelsea. Then you're at the funeral when Father O'Neil gets shot. Now you're here."

"I was investigating James Tully. That's why I was at his wife's funeral. When he received a death threat, it seemed pretty obvious he wasn't the guy. I came here for answers, but Clayton got to him before I could finish with my questions."

"And you didn't think at any point it might be time to turn this case over to the police?" Cohen said.

I looked at my hands. "It crossed my mind."

"I believe you're probably telling the truth," Lindsay said. "But you have to understand, we're going to need you to back off the case. Because of the way it looks. I'll pay you for what you've done for me. That's only right. But you need to let us take it from here."

I set my glass on the end table and stood up. "It's all yours," I said. "Make the check out to Nick Dioli, Investigative Services, and feel free to be creative with the 'for' line."

I started for the door, but they hadn't moved James' body yet. I hadn't exactly liked the guy, but I was looking at a relatively innocent man who'd died scared, while I listened from a few feet away.

"An officer will drive you down to the station to give a statement," Cohen said.

I didn't turn around. "Didn't I just give one? And, anyways, I called a cab right after I called you."

"Make your way to the station in the next half hour or I'll come find you," Cohen said.

I made my way to Kimmy's.

She was sitting behind the bar reading that thick book again. Otherwise I had the place to myself.

"Back to business as usual?" I said, taking my seat at the end of the bar.

She marked her place in the book with an old envelope, set it under the bar, and walked over with a bottle. "It's noon," she said, filling a glass.

I checked my cell: 12:15. I shrugged. "Well, it's—"

"If you say it's 5:00 somewhere, you'll die here today."

I closed my mouth. Then I opened it, shot my drink, and slid the glass forward. "Guess you hear that one a lot."

"I'm sorry," she said, filling my glass. "Studying and working and studying while working...it's got me tearing my hair out."

"I didn't know you were back in school."

She stared at me and blinked. "I've been studying for the bar exam for the last three months," she said.

I looked around the bar, my glass held up in front of me. I was at that blissful stage of inebriation where you say the things you normally wouldn't say in sensitive situations, and the recipient of your comments forgives you because they know it's the drink talking. "Bar exam? You've certainly had plenty of practice."

But Kimmy wasn't in a forgiving mood. She stared at me, and as I looked into her eyes with a no doubt idiotic expression on my face, I began to realize I was not, in fact, in that invincible state of inebriation just yet; and I was aware of sudden, lurking danger, as Kimmy reached under the bar. I fully expected a shotgun blast to rip through the bar and take my lap outside. But she stood up and twisted the cap off a cold bottle of water and set it on the bar top.

"Drink that," she said. "I'll make some coffee."

"I don't want coffee," I said.

"You need coffee," she said. "Then you're going to tell me what's up."

She made the coffee and I drank it dutifully. After a few minutes, I was explaining to her the situation at James' house.

When I was done, she stood there quietly a moment, leaning on the bar. "I can't believe James is dead."

I nodded.

She cleared her throat, turned and looked at the clock over the back of the bar. "So you've got about five minutes before RoboCop kicks in my door looking for you?"

I shrugged, sipping at my coffee. My head was still floating, but I was miserably aware of the thoughts moving through my mind. "He's just showing me how far he can piss," I said. "I'll get there when I get there."

"Clashing egos," she said, pulling her stool over to my side of the bar. She grabbed herself a bottle of water, twisted off the cap, and sat down. "Oh, how I wish I was a man." She took a long drink of her water, put the cap back on the bottle and set it down on the bar. "So you're really off the case?"

I nodded. "I'm paid."

"You can just let it go?"

"Easily," I said. "I'd always rather be here with you, though I'd rather not be drinking coffee."

"That's sad," she said.

I shrugged. "It's only half true."

"I had a feeling," she said.

I smiled. "You gonna ask which half is true?"

"I know," she said.

I finished up my coffee and she refilled my cup.

"So what's your next move?" she said.

"I don't know. To be honest, dropping the case is hard, and it's not because of some heightened sense of duty—don't think that. It's just...curiosity, I guess. I've got leads on Grimely and BB and T I'd like to follow up on. But I can't work for free. And from here on that's what I'd be doing."

"So then you *are* off the case?"

"I'm off it," I said. "It's just not easy to let it go."

"The cops don't even want you on as a consult for what you know?"

"Lindsay knows everything I know," I said, and I told her about Lindsay.

Her eyes narrowed. "Lindsay, huh? What's she look like?"

I finished up my coffee like a good boy. "She's a dog," I said.

"Uh-huh." She looked at me a moment, looked away, and then kind of glanced up again, like she was rolling an idea around in her head. I didn't like the look. "That cemetery where Cat's buried," she started, and I interrupted her.

"I know, crappy first date. I understand if you don't want to give me another chance."

103

"That's not what I was going to say."

"How's Jeffy?" I said, taking a sip of coffee.

"Nick…"

"Let's not," I said, looking at her.

"Stop trying to derail this conversation," she said. "You know where it's going. We've never talked about it in any real way, and if you've never talked about it with me, then it's a safe bet you've never talked about it."

"Some things are better left untalked-about," I said.

She looked at me for a long time. She had a way of doing that that made me feel like my fly was down.

"Was that the cemetery where Nancy's buried?" she asked.

I didn't answer. It *was* the cemetery where my wife was buried, but I hadn't let myself think about it then, and I didn't want to think about it now. My dead wife: not a topic that spent much time on the tip of my tongue. I'm more of a dirty jokes and big boobs guy, when it comes to passing time. Kimmy was a dredging-up-the-hurt-so-you-can-exercise-the-soul kind of girl. She was probably right. In fact, I truly believe she was. I needed to talk to somebody. Everyone I had talked to about Nancy's passing had a glass mouth, if you get what I mean. And all that pain was just wrapped around my stomach, tightening. You've felt it, I'm sure.

"Don't be upset," she said. "I just worry about you."

"You think about me when I'm not around?" I said, grinning. The grin took effort.

She rolled her eyes. "You need to go sleep it off."

"Alone?"

She grinned and looked away. "Feeling a little bolder than usual?" she said.

"I guess that's what sobriety does to me," I said, holding up my coffee. "Fill this up with JD, and you'll have your timid teddy bear back in no time."

"I wouldn't go that far," she said.

I smiled. "No. But hey, you can't say I'm a boring date—

drunk or sober."

"That's for sure," she said, smiling.

I watched that smile a second, and, pushing thoughts of Nancy from my mind, I said, "Come to think of it, I owe you a proper date."

"You do?"

I shrugged. "Considering that our first date was a funeral, and included an attempted murder, I think it's only right I take you out for a legitimate dinner. Maybe even a movie."

"Do you even watch movies?" she said.

"Old ones, mostly," I said, sipping my coffee.

She looked at me a moment, and suddenly I didn't want to let her finish. I didn't want to watch her struggle to find a kind way to tell me the thing I should already know. That she was too good for me.

"I don't feel like going out," she said.

I shrugged and finished off my coffee. "I'm broke anyways," I said, doing a bad job of hiding my disappointment.

"So, why don't you come to my house tonight and I'll fix us dinner."

I looked at her and tried to hide my genuine surprise. "I'd like that."

"Good," she said, getting to her feet. "Now go give the cops your statement so we don't spend date number two staring at each other through bars."

Chapter Ten

I rode down to the station in a cab and gave my official statement. It took two hours. After that I went to the office. Josh was doing squats with a resistance band tucked under his feet, a grip in each hand. He didn't immediately notice me, and when he did he let the handles snap to the floor and slipped into his chair. He didn't attempt to appear as if he'd been working. He just sat there with his hands placed flat on his desk, breathing heavily. His face was bright red, and the veins of his neck stood out like rivers on a map.

"Don't mind me," I said. "It looks like, for the moment, we both have some free time on our hands."

He looked at me, and his body relaxed. "You solved the case?"

"Don't sound so surprised," I said. "And no. Handed it off to the cops." I crossed to his desk and picked up the resistance band. I quickly realized I didn't know what I was doing with it, and dropped it to the floor.

"I thought you had a rule against that?"

I shook my head and sat on the end of his desk. "Didn't have a choice. But, honestly, you won't hear me complaining. I'm looking forward to the same old quiet jobs I normally do. I thought I hated that stuff. Thought I wanted excitement, to prove I still had whatever it was I used to have." I shrugged and shook my head. I was looking at my hands, which no longer had blood on them. I saw I was twisting the ring on my finger again and stuffed one hand into the pocket of my jacket. I ran the other hand through my hair and tried to think of what I was going to do to kill the rest of the day.

"Kimmy called," Josh said.

I looked at him. "Why didn't she call my cell?" I pulled my cell and saw that she had, in fact, called me four times and had left three text messages.

Josh smiled. "Anyways, she said Jeffy will have to join you guys tonight. Maggie's out of town."

I nodded. "Anything else?"

"You got a call from a Detective Cohen." Josh picked up a torn shred of paper and squinted at it. "He wanted to make sure you know not to leave town."

I laughed and, walking into my inner office, I said, "Why would I leave Charleston? Today, I own it."

I knew he didn't know what I meant by that and I didn't care. I sat at my desk and thought about my upcoming date with Kimmy.

That lasted a whole five minutes. Then I had to get out of there. I called Roald's office to set up a meeting. I was off the case. That hadn't changed. But I also had time to kill, and I'd rather be doing something than nothing. If I found something that might help Lindsay and Cohen, I'd make sure they paid me a little extra for it. If I found nothing, at least I wouldn't have died of boredom.

His office was out in Ladson, but he was currently doing a walk-through of the old library site off King, which was only a couple of blocks from my office. I headed out into the hot afternoon with my shirt tucked in and my jacket buttoned. I figured if I was going through the trouble of talking to him, I should command as much respect as possible, seeing as I was about to accuse his underling of conspiracy to commit murder.

I'd only had two drinks before I left my office, so I was feeling bold and confident, without the usual accompanying dizziness.

When I reached the site, I knew Roald immediately. He was the one standing just off the loose clay on the sidewalk in a full suit, gesturing heatedly toward a man driving a bulldozer. Two other men in orange vests and yellow helmets had turned away from him, laughing. As I got closer, I could see why. His voice was high and shrill, and seemed to come not from his throat, but from the small space between his lips and teeth.

"Mr. Ester," I said, stopping a few feet away from him.

He turned toward me and squinted, his hand still raised toward the man in the bulldozer.

"Help you?" he said.

I showed him my investigator's license. "Just a couple of questions."

Normally, when I flash the badge, I get a trademark look of disrespect—a subtle mix of sympathy and outright disdain. But he kept his eyes on the badge a moment, and then met my eyes with a serious expression. He lowered his arm and straightened his jacket. His large head glistened with sweat, and his eyes seemed too small and close-together for his face. It was the sort of physical characteristic that suggests a possible mental defect.

"This way," he said with a hint of alarm in his voice.

He started across the work site toward a trailer at the opposite end. The trailer door was open, and a small oscillating fan stood on a desk just inside. A broad, sunburned man sat behind the desk with his stubbly chin in one thick hand, his other hand clenched around a bottled water, dripping with condensation. When he saw us, he got to his feet with a groan and addressed Roald.

"Boiling out here," he said.

Roald looked back out the door as if the air itself might in fact be boiling, and then turned back to the man. "I don't know what you mean," he said. "Can we have the room?"

The man looked at me and his lips went up to one side in a grin. "Yep," he said, eyes on me as he walked out the door.

Roald walked around the desk and sat where the large man had been. He took a bottled water from the mini-fridge next to the desk and did not offer me one. He unscrewed the cap, took a sip, and then set the bottle down. He took a Kleenex from a box on the desk, wiped his lips. Then he balled up the tissue and tossed it onto the floor. Once he'd done this and burped twice, he looked up at me and said in his hi-pitched voice, "So what's this about?"

"James," I said. I watched him for a reaction.

He stared back at me as if I were dripping down a wall.

"James' murder," I said for clarification.

His nostrils flared as his eyes opened up wide. "James? Which James? My James?" He stood up and kept one hand on the desk, as if for balance. His wide eyes stayed on me.

"James Tully," I said. "He was shot this afternoon by a man named John Clayton."

Roald looked at me another moment. His thin mustache was beaded with sweat. His eyes fell away, and he shook his head slowly. "You say he was murdered?"

"Yes."

"How do you know?"

"I was there," I said. "I saw it happen, went after the shooter, but he got away."

Roald sat back down and rested his elbows on the desk. He crossed his arms and gripped his shoulders, as if he were suddenly cold.

For a moment, I didn't say anything. There was something off about Roald, and already I had trouble seeing him as the type to run a successful business. I gave him a moment, which he seemed to need, then I said, "I need you to tell me what your association was with James."

He shook his head and dropped his hands to the desk. "He's my friend," he said. He looked at me. "I've known James for years."

"So you would have known about his affair?"

He pulled his hands back and wiped them down the front of his jacket, bringing them to rest on his knees. He looked up at me and tried on a series of expressions, each one a poor attempt at shielding what seemed to be a growing sense of panic. "Why would you ask me that?"

"Because James was having an affair. And, as you said, you've known him for years. You must have seen the signs. You must have noticed that he and Cat were having problems."

"No marriage is perfect," he said, running a hand through his sparse hair. "Believe me."

"Are you and Gladys having trouble?"

He looked at me. "How do you know my wife?"

"The newspaper," I said. "That and because she was in my office not two days ago claiming to have witnessed Cat's murder."

He stood up and let the chair roll back into the wall. "That's a lie."

"I've got her report filed away," I said. "She claims James shoved Cat off the pier."

"That's ridiculous," he said.

"I know."

He watched me and his large round face turned red. "What are you insinuating? That my wife is somehow responsible for Cat's death?"

I shook my head. "Nothing like that. I know Cat's death was an accident, and I'm sure Gladys misunderstood what she saw." I sat on the edge of the desk and tried to put on a more amicable face. "The real reason I'm here is to see what you know about Grimely and his crew of ex-cons."

He shook his head and exhaled an exasperated breath that turned into a pinched laugh. "Grimely's my hapless cousin," Roald said. He sat down and folded his hands on the desk.

"Hapless?" I said. "He seems to run a solid business."

Roald laughed again. "He has a solid business because I hire him to do my jobs and I stay on top of his men to see that the jobs are done properly."

"Why help him if you don't want to?"

"He's my cousin on my mother's side," Roald said with a monotone apathy that told me he'd gone over this before.

"And you want to keep Mom happy," I said.

He nodded.

I looked back out the door. The broad man who had just left was about twenty feet from the trailer, laughing with two of the men Roald had been grilling when I first arrived.

"That him?" I said.

Roald nodded. "Yep." He shook his head with disgust.

I leaned over the desk. "Why would he want to conceal James' affair?"

Roald stared at me. "Do what now?"

I shrugged and got to my feet. I unbuttoned my jacket and paced the floor, thinking. After a moment, I walked over and sat on the edge of the desk, leaning toward him again. I glanced toward Grimely, and then turned back to Roald to show him I was on his side. "The man who killed James and shot Father O'Neil works for your cousin."

Roald's eyes widened and then his face went lax. His eyes moved back and forth over the table as if he'd misplaced something. Then he rested his hand over his mouth and exhaled a long breath that caused his cheeks to flutter. "I was sorry to hear about Father O'Neil," he said.

"Me too," I said.

"I don't understand your question," he said.

"Why would your cousin be willing to kill James and Father O'Neil to keep James' affair a secret?"

Silence a moment, and then, "I don't follow."

I didn't know how much I wanted to tell him. For all I knew he was complicit with his cousin's activities, if his cousin was the one calling the shots. But five minutes with him had shown me that he was gullible, insecure, and generally unstable. In my experience, that meant as long as I was persistent I could at least get what he did know, if anything. So, I told him part of it: "James and Cat were seeing Father O'Neil for counseling about the affair. At the funeral, James gets a note that says simply, 'Keep quiet or this is you.' Ten minutes later, Father O'Neil has a bullet in his chest."

"Okay."

"I think the warning, if spelled out in its entirety would have read, 'keep quiet about the affair or this is you.'"

"But didn't you say James was killed this afternoon?" Roald said.

"Yeah."

"Did he talk? I mean, what's the point in making an elaborate threat if you're just going to kill the man a day later?"

I looked at him, then I got up from the desk and started pacing again. It was a good question and it pointed out a gaping hole in my theory as to the killer's motivation. James had talked to me, sure, but who knew that? Clayton could have had eyes on me since the funeral. Maybe even before. Gladys had spotted me, after all. If Clayton had had eyes on James, he could have seen us talking at the hospital, but he couldn't have known what we'd been talking about. So, why had he decided to kill James? Paranoia? Whoever he was reporting to might have gotten jumpy, decided to get rid of everyone who knew about the affair just to be sure. But that only made a bigger mess. Whatever they were trying to cover up by burying the affair could be at greater risk of being exposed as the body count climbed. Murder, after all, draws even the legitimate papers.

"He talked to me," I said. "Other than that, I don't know."

Roald stared at me, and the look in his eyes told me I might have misjudged him. He was more perceptive than he initially let on.

"You best watch your back then," he said. "Whoever it is. But, I have to say, you're wrong about my cousin."

"How do you know?"

"He has no reason to cover up James' affair. He's a drunken half-wit who would be a homeless drunken half-wit if not for me. I don't think he's ever even met James."

"So, Grimely and James aren't connected in any way?" I said. "You're sure?"

He nodded. "They move in very different circles."

I thought about that a moment, thanked him for his time, and left.

It was around 6:00 when I headed home to shower and get ready for my date with Kimmy. I was dehydrated and my head felt like a bruise; but mostly I felt good. Roald and Grimely had been my last two leads. I'd spoken with Grimely briefly after leaving Roald, but he'd offered nothing useful, other than to corroborate what Roald had said about his relationship with James—that there wasn't one. I didn't know who was controlling John Clayton, but the police would catch up with him soon enough. There was nothing else for me to do. The case had weighed on me heavily, and it was a relief to hand it off to the cops half done. It was rare I could do that and still get paid. I was thinking this, and even had a smile on my face, when I reached the second floor landing of my apartment complex to find Virginia and Chelsea standing outside my door.

Neither of them said a word. Virginia had a hand on Chelsea's shoulder, and they both stared at me. It was like an image from one of those commercials calling for donations to feed the hungry. I stood there silently. Then I barked out a laugh that died flat. There was no humor in it. I felt my short-lived sense of relief drain out of me, and I was filled back up with lead.

I took my keys from my pocket, and the vagrants parted silently as I approached my door, unlocked it, and went inside. I left the door open behind me and went straight to the kitchen. I took the bottle from the cabinet over the stove and a 16 oz tumbler from another cabinet. The front door snapped shut. I filled the tumbler half way and shot a fourth of it. I stayed there, leaning on the counter, not looking back toward the entrance to the kitchen, where I knew they now stood, staring at me with that lost puppy expression on their faces.

"Is James really dead?" Virginia said.

I nodded slowly, still not turning around.

There was a short pause, and then: "Was it you?"

"God almighty," I said, turning to face them now. "You too?"

She drew Chelsea closer. "I'm not here to judge," she said. "If you did it, I won't blame you."

I leaned back against the counter, shaking my head. I wanted to take my disappointment and all of the rest of my frustrations out on her, but that wouldn't have been fair. It wasn't their fault, entirely, that some mad man was out to kill them. I just wished they'd take their problems somewhere else. The cop in me had gone back to sleep, and that's the way I wanted it.

I shook my head, and I didn't look up at her or speak again until I was cool enough to do it without shouting.

"You guys hungry?" I said.

Chelsea nodded.

I heated up three TV dinners, the last of my food for the week, and we sat in the living room, all crammed on my sofa, and ate over the coffee table. I had a small TV balanced on a nightstand across the room, and no cable. The only DVD I had was a copy of the *RoboCop* remake, so we watched that while I caught them up on the case.

When I finished, I noticed they had stopped eating. Chelsea's eyes were moist, and run-through with intersecting red lines. Virginia had placed a hand on Chelsea's back and was rubbing up and down vigorously. "Mom slipped?" Chelsea said.

I nodded. "That's what your dad told me," I said.

"You just took his word for it?" Virginia said. She was having the same problem Lindsay had at first, accepting that James wasn't the killer they'd suspected him to be. Only, Lindsay had come around to the truth with a little less stubborn denial.

"It wasn't just his word," I said, setting down my fork. "I got the feeling something wasn't right from the moment I started looking into him. My source couldn't find any dirt on him, and he seemed genuinely crushed over Cat's death. Then he received the death threat, and Father O'Neil got shot, and it became clear something more was going on here."

Chelsea dropped her face into her hands. She sobbed heavily. Virginia hugged her close, kissing the top of her head and telling her it would be OK.

I sat there a moment silently, not sure what to say. Then I said, "Your father understood, Chelsea. He didn't hold it against you."

"I accused him of murder," she said without lifting her head. "I wasn't here when he buried Mom." She shook her head with her hands still covering her face. She looked at Virginia, and then at me. "How could I be so stupid? He was trying to save her, and I accused him of killing her."

"It's OK," Virginia said, kissing the top of her head again. She pulled Chelsea's head down against her breast and looked at me. She shook her head softly, and the look in her eyes told me she didn't know what to do or say either. I'll admit, in all of this, I hadn't even considered how it would be for Chelsea when she found out her mother's death was a freak accident, and that her Father had died knowing he was outside her good graces.

"You're father understood," I said. "He told me so."

She lifted her head and looked at me. She wiped her nose, and ran a forearm across her eyes.

I went on. "He said it was dark, and he knew how things must have looked from the shore. He said he knew why you were upset and he loved you all the more for it."

"No he didn't," she said, but I saw the flicker of relief on her face, in the sudden erect posture of her back, and I kept telling my lie.

"He did," I said. "He said he was proud of you for standing up for your mother the way you did. He said he couldn't imagine having a better daughter. All he cared about was making sure you were safe."

She wiped her nose on her sleeve and looked at me. Then she looked at Virginia. Virginia smiled, her eyes red and wet, and nodded her head. "I think he's telling the truth," she said.

Chelsea looked at me again, and then down at the floor.

"Can I ask you something?" I said.

Chelsea nodded without looking up.

"This might be hard, but it's important."

She looked at me and waited.

"Do you know about your father's affair?"

"Good God," Virginia said.

"It's important," I said.

"What affair?" Virginia said. "What are you talking about?"

I looked at her. "James was sleeping with another woman," I said. "It's why he and Cat were having problems."

"Christ," she said, hugging Chelsea close. "Does she need to hear about it now, after all this?"

"I already know," Chelsea said.

The room was quiet a moment. I heard tires rolling over gravel outside.

"What?" Virginia said, holding the girl away so she could look at her.

"I knew about Dad's affair." She looked away.

"Do you know the woman he was cheating with?" I said. I had cast off all notions of sensitivity.

Chelsea kept her eyes on the floor and gave no indication she'd heard me.

"Do you know the woman?" I repeated.

She nodded her head slowly.

I watched her, transfixed. I was afraid to say anything more, as if she was caught under some spell that could be broken by my own eagerness.

She took a deep breath and looked at me, and the expression on her face was that of a brand new person, freshly shoved into adulthood. "My babysitter," she said, and her eyes didn't move. "Jessica. She told me I could call her Jess."

I stared at her a moment as if she hadn't yet spoken. And then, slowly, I began to feel the blood moving through my face. My scalp tingled. Water brimmed along the lower lids of my eyes. And once I was aware she'd spoken, and the words had finally registered, I realized I was embarrassed. Embarrassed I hadn't thought of it. The babysitter. She was the connection. And who did that point too? Who had the most to lose if the affair was exposed?

I got to my feet quickly, and my hands were balled into fists. I'd felt the smile break across my face when there was a knock at the door. Three knocks actually—slow and firm.

I wasn't expecting anyone.

I turned to Virginia and Chelsea, who sat on the couch staring up at me as if I'd just come in through the chimney. I pointed toward the hallway leading back to my bedroom. "Get to the room," I said. I'd set my jacket and holster on the back of a dining room chair, just off the entryway to the apartment. I went for it, and my hand was on the butt of my gun when the door burst open, and John Clayton walked in with his own gun raised.

"Hands off," he said. He held the gun on me as he pressed the door shut. He'd busted the latch, so it hung open slightly. I could hear Rivers Avenue traffic, and the laughter of tenants on the lower floor. "Back," he said. A red and white Atlanta Braves hat covered his bald head. He wore a white t-shirt, blue jeans, and tan, soiled work boots. He tracked clumps of red clay on the carpet as he stepped toward me.

I slowly let my hand fall to my side and backed away from the gun. He pointed the nose of his gun toward the couch.

I had my hands in the air as I backed toward the couch. I stopped beside the coffee table. "Grimely's making you work day and night, huh?"

"What?"

I nodded toward his boots. "I figured with all the after-hours work he's got you doing, he might let you sleep in days."

"After hours?" he said, and then a smile spread across his face. "Oh, you mean the killings? Got nothing to do with Grimely. Sit."

I knew it didn't have anything to do with Grimely; but, in my experience, playing dumb's the best way to get people to divulge their secrets. I sat down on the couch and set my hands in my lap.

"If not Grimely, then who?" I said. "It was awfully kind of Grimely to offer two fugitives a steady job. It would make a lot more sense if it were worth his risk."

"I'm not here to talk about work," he said.

"Well, what are you waiting for?" I said. "You shot James the second he opened the door. Now you're taking time out to make sure I'm comfortable. I know what James knew. So, what's the hold up?"

"Shut up and sit quiet," he said with the gun trained on me. He slipped a pack of cigarettes from his back pocket and coaxed one out with his lips. He put the pack back in his pocket and pulled out a lighter. He lit the cigarette and tossed the lighter onto the coffee table. It landed next to Chelsea's barely touched TV dinner. John dragged the cigarette, then pinched it between two fingers and blew out smoke. He watched the table through the screen of smoke a moment, then spat on the floor. He didn't look at me as he said, "You eating for three?"

I kept my face neutral and my voice even. "Been meaning to clean up. If only I'd known you'd be dropping by."

He shook his head and approached the table. He touched the food in each container. "It's all still warm," he said, wiping his fingers on his pants. "Who's here?"

There was gunfire from the TV across the room, as RoboCop took out a warehouse full of bad guys. He looked at the TV, then back at me. "You got me," I said. "A couple of my associates were just here, helping me work on a case."

He grinned. "What case is that?"

"Some asshole's been going around killing people to make some fat guy with bad facial hair happy," I said.

"You think Roald's pulling the strings?" Clayton said.

"He's got the money," I said. "And he's got something to lose if word gets out his niece was sleeping with James."

"I was paid days ago," he said.

"I guess that makes you one loyal gunman," I said. "Why not just take the money and run?"

He was distracted, backing up to peek around the wall into the kitchen, then taking a few steps toward the hallway, listening. After a moment of standing quietly with his ear cocked toward the hallway, he looked at me. "No one's left this apartment since you got here," he said.

I looked at him, and I felt the grin spreading on my own face. I crossed one leg over the other and leaned back on the couch, slipping my hand into the pocket where my cell phone was. "You've been following me."

"Thought you'd never come home," he said. He leaned over the coffee table and plucked a square of Salisbury steak from one of the TV dinner containers and ate it. He made a face as he chewed.

"You still haven't explained to me why I'm alive," I said.

His eyes remained on the food containers. "An associate of mine seems to think Chelsea isn't at the bakery anymore."

He looked at me. "I thought, before I kill you, you might be so kind as to tell me where she is."

"What makes you think I would know?"

He backed toward the dining room table, watching me. He dragged the chair that wore my gun holster and jacket into the living room. He sat on the opposite side of the coffee table with the gun aimed at my chest. "I know James sent you out there to get Chelsea and bring her home. I know you figured out someone else had come for Chelsea before, and I know you know that somebody was a friend of mine."

"Michael," I said. "How's he doing?"

His body tensed, but he kept a glint of humor in his eyes. "I know you know about Michael. I think you know how he died."

I shook my head. "I know the cops are looking into it, but I haven't heard anything."

He made a sound like a popped soda cap. "It was the old lady. We both know that. I told Michael to be smart about it. As you can see, he didn't listen too well."

"A good partner in crime is hard to find," I said.

"Call them out," he said. His grin spread.

"What?"

"Call them out here," he said. "Come on. Don't make me go find them."

"I don't know what you're talking about," I said. And just then my cell began to vibrate. I watched him, trying not to give anything up through the expression on my face. I felt for the "accept call" button, pressed it, and hoped whoever was on the other end didn't hang up. "I don't know what you're talking about," I said, more loudly now. "There's nobody here."

He held his smile. "Why don't I just pop you right now, then go check for myself?" He raised his gun level with my eyes.

"I've already called the police." John and I both looked toward the hallway to see Virginia. She was standing in the

121

entryway, her long gray hair falling over her shoulders, those blue eyes turned to stone again, the way they'd looked when I first met her. I'd hoped she and the girl had gone out a window, but I was also appreciative of the fact I hadn't yet been shot.

"We won't be here that long," John said. "Bring the girl out here."

"No," Virginia said.

He looked at me and his smile was gone. "What is it with you people?" he said. "I've got a gun." He shrugged and waved the gun in the air. "Do I have to clarify that every time I make a request? Let me be clear." He stood up and kicked the chair over. It hit the floor in front of the coffee table, and the gun holster slipped off and landed under the table. He had his gun aimed at Virginia. "If you don't get the girl out here, I'll shoot both of you with this gun." He looked back and forth between us, pointing at the gun with his free hand. "Boom boom—do you see? Then I'll walk down the hallway and get the girl myself."

"That's what you'll have to do if you want to take her," Virginia said.

He looked at me with an expression of mild shock, turned to Virginia and took a step toward her, gun aimed at her head.

I slipped off the couch and placed the palms of my hands on the underside of the coffee table, lifting it as I stood up. He had turned just enough to see it coming as I threw the coffee table and it struck his upper body. He caught it instinctively and lost his balance, falling back, knocking the TV from its stand and falling to the floor. Virginia ran back down the hallway. I dropped to the floor, slipped my gun from its holster, and was getting to my feet again when I heard the shot. Something shattered on the shelf above the sofa, and I took a long step to the right and trained my gun on John, who'd already gotten to his knees. Blood ran from his lips as he grinned, and took aim.

Whiskey for Breakfast

I fired. It caught him in the left shoulder, and the force of the bullet brought him to his feet and back against the opposite wall. He stumbled, but didn't drop. He shot again, this time from the waist, and I felt the bullet hit where my right thigh meets the hip. I twisted and fell back onto an end table. I balanced there long enough to take aim and pop off another shot. It hit him center chest. His arms flailed out to either side, as if he were about to make a declaration of love, and he dropped to his knees. He was still grinning as he went down. I slid to the floor and lost my grip on my gun. My pants were soaked through with blood. My vision went blurry, and then I was out.

When I woke up Lindsay was kneeling next to me with a bath towel jammed against my hip with two tight fists. She leaned in, looked directly into my eyes and said, "An ambulance is on the way. Try to stay awake until they get here."

She had blood on her arms, and a smear of it on her right cheek. I figured she must have been the one who called my cell while I was hashing it out with Clayton.

"Thank you," I said, and my voice sounded like it was coming from outside. She was focused on keeping pressure on my wound and didn't respond. I saw that Chelsea and Virginia were standing just outside the hallway, side by side with that please-donate-a-dollar look on their faces.

I looked at Lindsay again. "Why'd you call?"

She had her teeth gritted with effort. "Checking to see if it was a good time to continue our discussion."

A bolt of pain shot up my side. I clenched my teeth and shut my eyes. When the pain lessened I took a few quick breaths and said, "We definitely need to talk."

"Not now," she said, and that's all I remember of that night.

Chapter Eleven

I woke up twenty-four hours later in Roper Hospital, two rooms down from where Father O'Neil had been staying. I had memories of coming in and out of consciousness over the course of the last day, and seeing Kimmy and Josh and Lindsay; and now, as I came to full consciousness for the first time, I remembered asking about father O'Neil and finding out that he'd died in surgery. The pang of regret at hearing of his death was the first emotion to greet me as I blinked my eyes drunkenly against the bright lights of the room. The shades had been pulled back from the window to the left of my bed, and I could see the vague outline of someone seated in front of it. The figure stirred, and I heard the rattle of a magazine tossed aside.

A moment later my vision had mostly cleared, and I could see that the figure was Gladys Ester.

"You lied," I said, and my voice sounded distant and weak. It took her a moment to respond, but when she did her voice sounded the same.

"In more ways than you know," she said.

I could see now that she was dressed in a red blouse and a pair of white slacks, and she had a leather bag in her lap, gripped in both hands as if she carried every cent of her husband's fortune in it. Her metal cane leaned against the chair. Her eyes looked raw from crying. I wasn't about to consider those tears were for me. "Your niece," I said, and a wave of dizziness washed the rest of my sentence away.

She nodded. "Yes."

The room was quiet. I listened to it for a while, and she waited. I got the sense she was here to be questioned. She had a burden to unload.

I said, "You or Roald?"

"I just wanted everything to go away," she said.

"So you figured, if everyone involved was dead, that would about do it?"

She shook her head. "I didn't want anyone to die." A nurse passed by the door, and Gladys looked up, startled, and waited another moment before she continued. When she spoke again, her voice was nearly a whisper. "That was Roald. He said we should kill James, Chelsea and the priest, just to be safe. I said that was ridiculous. I told him it would simply draw more attention to our situation."

"And that situation, you mean the fact your niece had been knocked up by a local judge?"

She looked down at her lap and fiddled with the strap of her purse. When she had put the words together the way she wanted to say them, she looked up at me and said, "Roald's been working on his downtown project for ten years. Ten years. His reputation as a good businessman, a visionary, and a good Christian, is all that has shielded him from the army of preservationists trying to stall his work indefinitely." She looked at the doorway again and then down into her lap. "If word were to surface of Jessica's indiscretion..." She looked up at me.

"Roald would lose the few backers he has," I said.

She nodded. "His friends on the city council; his private investors; the downtown residents who are tired of their daughters getting attacked in the night by homeless perverts—they'd all go away, afraid to stand behind a man who would dare to claim such a noble goal while all the time keeping a harlot in his very own home."

"I don't know," I said, feeling my head clear as a dull, throbbing pain began to grow in my hip. I still couldn't move. "There's a lot of money to be made, jumping on board with Roald, especially as an investor. Much like you and your husband, the rich are often fully willing to turn a blind eye toward indiscretion when it serves their wallets."

"We talked about that," she said, nodding. "But decided we couldn't risk it, not after ten years. You have to understand, there's no starting over, and if this project fails, there's nothing waiting for us but a few more bland years."

I watched her a moment. "So your first lie was saying you saw James kill Cat."

"Yes," she said. "Mind you, I saw some of what happened. I saw them run out onto that pier. I saw Chelsea run from her father. But it was too dark and overcast to see what happened between James and Cat on the end of that pier. I told you that because I thought, if James was in prison he wouldn't have to die."

"Sending someone to prison's a piss poor way to shut'em up," I said. "You're begging for a snitch."

"That's what Roald said. But I happen to know that James was in love with Jessica, and he would not have done or said anything to put her life or comfort in jeopardy."

I thought about James' refusal to let me speak with Jessica, to know anything about her. "So you figured he'd be too afraid to rat you out because, what, it would hurt Jessica's reputation?"

"There was that," she said. "And the money as well. Jessica's future is as firmly tied to Roald's projects as mine. If James told the police the truth, that I had falsely accused him of murder to keep him from seeing Jessica and from talking about their affair, he would have ruined Jessica's life. I believe he would have kept quiet."

"But Roald wasn't so sure."

She shook her head. "I convinced him we could bring Chelsea back alive and make her stay quiet. But I couldn't convince him to do the same with James. I even suggested paying James off, but he liked that idea even less."

"So Michael Williams didn't go to the bakery to kill Chelsea, but to kidnap her?"

She nodded. "He was supposed to use his discretion with anyone else who happened to be in the room, but Chelsea was to be brought home alive."

"As for the second lie," I said. "Why did Father O'Neil have to die?"

Her eyes shined with moisture. "Roald wanted him dead, just in case. But I stopped John Clayton before he got too far, offered him double pay if he let Father O'Neil live."

"What happened?"

"Shortly after, John heard about Michael's death. He and Michael were lifelong friends, and he went berserk once he found out. The task became less a matter of money and more a matter of revenge for him. At that point, it didn't matter who it was, he seemed to want to kill everyone, the whole world." She put her face in her hands. "I couldn't control him."

"Money only gets you so far when you're dealing with psychos," I said.

She lifted her head, and tears streaked her wrinkled cheeks. She nodded and said, "That's why I came here today. I wanted to confess everything to you." She looked at me. "I truly hoped you wouldn't die. I couldn't stand to have another life on my conscience."

"I bet it's been exhausting," I said.

"Why do you say it like that?" she said. "I'm only asking for a little understanding."

"You might be asking too much," I said. "But I don't know. Let's wait until the bullet hole in my hip heals, then we'll see."

Whiskey for Breakfast

Her face turned red, but it wasn't grief now—I'd struck a wrong chord. She wiped her eyes and sat up straight. "You have a fully deserved reputation as a brash, heartless drunk."

"I have a reputation?" I said.

She barked a sigh of exasperation and got to her feet with the purse hugged to her breast. She looked at me a moment, took her cane in hand, and started for the door.

"Just one second," I said.

She stopped and turned to face me.

"When I get out of here, I'm putting you and your husband away for murder."

Her mouth dropped open and she blinked. "After everything I just told you about how I tried to save their lives—you would..."

"I would," I said. "And I will." Another hot bolt of pain shot up my side, and I knew she saw it on my face.

She held her shocked expression another moment, and then it melted. And what was left was the chiseled look of resolve she'd worn on her visit to my office. I knew now it was the look she wore to hide some secret emotion. In this case, I got the feeling that emotion was fear. "Are you sure you want to present yourself as a threat?" She walked toward me, slipping her hand into her purse.

I figured she might have brought a gun with her, in case her confession didn't go over so well. But I wasn't too concerned over the possibility she'd use it on me in here. After all, I wasn't ringing the nurse's bell to rat her out this instant; I was giving her fair warning and a head start. But what she pulled from her purse wasn't a gun, it was a knife. It was long and narrow, with a small, decorative handle. It looked more like a letter opener. She walked toward me with it, and every step or so she'd stop and turn to walk away, then she'd keep coming. Her eyes begged me for forgiveness and she hadn't even done it yet. I lay there watching her get closer, knowing I couldn't do a thing about it. My arms were still too weak to come to my defense. Her hesitance gave me plenty of time to think over the idea of being stabbed to death by a frail old woman. I imagined her raising the knife over me, like some scene of sacrifice from the movies. There would be that moment of anticipation, then a tug of pain, and then...what? I figured there were two possibilities: reunion with my wife in a world of eternal light and peace or nothing. More than likely the latter. But that seemed preferable to the way my life had been going lately.

She was still moving toward me when I closed my eyes. The last thing I saw was the look of guilt on her face. And I had just about accepted death, the idea of release from my demons and all of my obligations—the ultimate hiding place—when I heard her let out a startled yelp. And I was so deep in my meditation that by the time I realized I wasn't dead and opened my eyes, Lindsay had entered the room, disarmed the old woman, and thrust her across my prone legs with her hands behind her back.

Lindsay cuffed her and jerked her to her feet. Then she looked at me. Her hair hung loose from a purple tie, and her face was flushed. "How many times do I have to save you?" she said breathlessly.

Chapter Twelve

I told Lindsay what Gladys had told me, and given the scene she'd walked in on, she didn't have any trouble accepting the truth of it. A full investigation was launched on the Ester family, and by the time I got out of the hospital, Roald and Gladys had been arrested and were being held without bail until their trial.

The first thing I did was go to Kimmy's and apologize for missing our date. The apology wasn't necessary, but I made it anyway—the knee-jerk reaction of a practiced asshole. We accepted that we would go on another date sometime in the future, but decided to wait until it felt right, and I was OK with that, I guess.

After I left Kimmy, I went home to find Lindsay, Chelsea and Virginia waiting for me. I didn't like the way Lindsay looked at me or the expression of guilt on Virginia's face. And when Lindsay said, "Why don't we go inside and have that discussion," I liked her tone of voice even less.

I unlocked the door and went for the kitchen. I was using a cane at the time, and I'd almost reached the bottle when Lindsay told me to leave it and sit down on the couch. I sat between Virginia and Chelsea. Chelsea's face was the hot, bloody red you see on a kid's face when she's about to cry. But

Chelsea was barely a kid anymore, and she kept the tears inside. Virginia clenched her hands in her lap, and something about seeing how frightened she was caused me to sweat.

Lindsay paced in front of us. I hadn't replaced the coffee table yet, and I hadn't tried to do anything about the blood either. There was still glass from the TV stuck in the carpet, and there were still holes in the wall. But she ignored all that, pacing, her boots crunching over the glass. After a moment she stopped and looked at me; by then my nerves were rattled and I barely knew why.

"Who shot Michael Williams," she said.

I looked back at her as coldly as I could manage. I felt Virginia begin to fold up next to me. "I don't know," I said.

Lindsay smiled. "We're past that," she said. She folded her arms and leaned her weight onto one leg. If it were anyone else, you could have seen right through the act. But I could tell, with Lindsay it was no act, the way she held that stance. Much like my office, she had now claimed my living room. I'm not ashamed to admit it. I've got worse things to be ashamed of than the mild apprehension I feel when faced with a fearless woman strapped with a gun.

Virginia stood up. "I did it," she said. I looked up at her, and her eyes were shining with moisture, but she put on a good, southern show of stubborn pride.

Lindsay kept her eyes on me, but there was a sudden stiffness to her posture. "That so?"

I held her glare a moment, and the hard expression on her face softened a little. Not much, but it was enough. "How long have you known?" I said.

"How long have *you* known?" she said.

"You couldn't have known since the bar," I said.

"I've known since I visited your office that you knew something."

"How's that?"

"You don't have the poker face you think you have." She looked at Virginia and her expression changed again. "I didn't know it was you though, Aunt V."

Virginia looked down at the floor, then at me, and then back up at Lindsay. "He burst into my shop in the middle of the night with a knife. What should I have done?"

"You were right in everything but moving the body," Lindsay said. "You should have left him where he fell and called me."

"I panicked," Virginia said, looking to me for help.

I didn't know what to say. My plan had been to not say anything and let Virginia skate. But Lindsay was understandably conflicted. Not only was her job at risk if the truth ever came out, but she risked her sense of self, her identity as an officer of the law, if she swept this under the rug.

I was about to speak when Chelsea got to her feet and hurried over to her grandmother's side. "She saved me," Chelsea said. "What does it matter if she moved the body? Are you really going to arrest her?" Chelsea was still doing a good job of keeping back her tears, but her voice broke a little.

Lindsay stared at Chelsea a moment, and I could see the war going on behind her eyes.

"Listen," I said. "At this point, your case has got nothing to do with me. But if you want some free advice, you need to get your stories straight before Gladys and Roald go to trial. Because they sent Michael out there to get Chelsea, and that's bound to come up in testimony. How he died might come up too."

"Why can't we just tell the truth?" Chelsea said.

I looked at Lindsay and shrugged. "You could, but Grandma will likely do time for hiding the body. It just looks bad, and it'd be tough to explain away."

"But she was confused," Chelsea said.

"We know that," I said. "But you've got to convince a jury."

There was quiet a moment.

"So, what do we do?" Lindsay said. She was looking at me. Everyone was.

I thought a moment. I rubbed my hand over my face and through my hair. Then I looked at Lindsay. "You need a fall guy."

Lindsay shook her head, but didn't say anything.

"Like who?" Virginia said. "I'll face what's coming to me before I'll convict an innocent person."

"Who said he had to be innocent?" I said. I told them what Gladys had told me about John Clayton, how he'd gone rogue and started killing just to kill. "All we have to do is modify the story a little," I said. I looked at Virginia. "Maybe John and Michael broke into your bakery. Maybe they got into a tiff and John shot Michael in a psychotic fit, and then regretted it. Blamed you. You put a couple rounds into the wall and he took off with the body."

Lindsay was still shaking her head. "I won't do that," she said.

I looked at her. "He was an animal."

"It doesn't matter," she said. "It's a slippery slope. Next thing you know I'll be fixing tickets and stealing money from evidence."

"But this is about family," Chelsea said. The tears had come now.

Lindsay looked at her, then back down at the floor, shaking her head harder now. "No," she said. "We'll have to take our chances."

"You don't have any," I said.

Lindsay looked at me. "Michael was as bad as John," she said. "It shouldn't be too hard to convince a jury of the truth."

"If you want to risk that," I said.

Lindsay looked at Virginia. Virginia had leaned back into the couch, looking at her hands resting in her lap.

Whiskey for Breakfast

I watched Lindsay's face soften some more. "John's dead," I said. "And one more murder on his rap sheet won't make a difference."

She looked at me, and I wasn't sure how to read her face.

A knock at the door.

We all turned toward the sound like scared mice caught in a shoebox. We sat quiet a moment, each of us hoping whoever it was would feel the gravity of our discussion and leave us to it. I could hear shoe leather scraping the cement landing as someone paced impatiently.

Another knock at the door. Harder this time.

"Open up, Dioli."

"Shit," Lindsay said in a harsh whisper.

I didn't have to ask. I'd only met Cohen a couple times, but I knew the voice.

"What did you tell him?" I said.

"Nothing," Lindsay said. She looked away. "Only that I knew you knew something."

Two more hard knocks.

"You do remember that you talked me into this case?" I said.

She looked at me. "It didn't take too much talking after I mentioned the pay."

I looked toward the door and then back at her. "The point is, I wouldn't be in this situation if I hadn't decided to help you. If Cohen finds out I knew about Michael's murder all along, that's it for me. Now I need you to help me, and in the process, help yourself and your family."

She shook her head and I grabbed her by the arm. She gave me that look she was so good at, but I was over it. I wasn't going to jail for her or her Aunt V. Not over a look.

"You're going to do it," I said.

"Please," Virginia said. She pressed her locked hands over her lips. Her eyes were big and wet. I let go of Lindsay's arm.

Lindsay held that look on me another moment, then turned to Virginia. Chelsea had fallen into deep sobs.

Three more hard knocks at the door. "Last warning," Cohen said. "Next time I knock, it's with my boot."

We were all looking at Lindsay now, but I couldn't wait for her answer. "Wipe the tears," I said to Chelsea as I got to my feet. I went to the front door with my intestines in a knot. Cohen was standing with his hand on the butt of his gun. He wore the same Kinko's manager outfit he'd been in the last time I'd seen him, and I had a sudden flash image in my head of a closet packed with well-pressed blue button-downs.

"Took you long enough," he said, pushing his way in. He stopped when he saw Virginia and Chelsea on the couch, and Lindsay standing opposite. Chelsea had stopped sobbing, but her eyes looked raw. Virginia had her hands clutched in her lap again, her mouth a stolid frown. Lindsay had her hands on her hips, and she was looking at Cohen as if he'd just kicked mud on her boots.

"The hell is going on here?" Cohen said.

"I might ask you the same," Lindsay said.

I stood off to the side, leaning against the partition that separated the living room from the entryway. I'd left my cane over by the couch. No way I'd let Cohen see me that way. But my hip was on fire.

"I hadn't heard from you," Cohen said. "I came over to make sure things were going Ok."

"We're fine," Lindsay said.

"Why didn't you answer?" Cohen said.

Lindsay kept her eyes on him, but I could see she was stumped.

"Weren't sure who it was," I said. "Last guy who busted through my door had bad intentions."

"Aren't you supposed to announce yourself as the police when you knock on a door?" Chelsea said. She was trying to sound confident, but her voice was still a little shaky.

Cohen looked at her. Then his eyes moved from Virginia to Lindsay to me. He grinned.

"Okay," he said, straightening his belt. "What did I walk in on?"

Quiet.

"Lindsay came over to question me," I said, my arms folded over my chest. I shrugged. "She was under the impression I knew something about Michael Williams."

He turned to me. "And do you?"

I shrugged again and looked at Lindsay.

Lindsay stared at me for a long time. But this look was new. And I understood what she was telling me, no words necessary. This look was an accusation, because I knew what she was giving up; and, most often, it *is* a slippery slope. Lindsay was a clean cop, still young, still bent on doing things by the book. But after today, much like Chelsea, she'd have moved beyond who she used to be. A little wiser, in a way— but mostly just colder. And I knew how gradual that coldness came, how it could sneak up on you. It had me now so that moments of levity came as a shocking reminder that I was still human. She had a long way to go before it got her that bad, but if she stayed in the business long enough, it would come.

She held that look a moment longer, then turned to Cohen. "John Clayton shot Michael Williams," she said.

Epilogue

It was months later. Roald and Gladys were awaiting sentencing, but it didn't look good for them. Gladys had tried her self-pity routine on the jury to ill effect. I'd healed up well enough, but still had to use the cane.

I got up one morning, had no cases pending, and headed out to where Father O'Neil had been buried. He was buried in an old family plot at a little place off Rivers Avenue. It took me a while to shuffle to his spot at the back corner along the woods. It was evening, and the heat was mild. There was a breeze, and I stood there looking down at his grave, maybe a little weepy from too much whiskey before I left the apartment, but I wouldn't say I was crying. I barely knew the man, after all. But there was something about him that had intrigued me, I guess you'd say. He'd woken something up inside me, and I'd been trying to figure out what that was. And I'd decided on something. It might have been that whole thing about confession. About how you can tell a priest what you did wrong and you get some relief from the guilt, and a weight lifts off your soul. I remembered the feeling from my Catholic school days. Going to confession every week with my dad. I'd walk into that cold room and the priest would be sitting behind a divider. All I could see of him were his shiny shoes poking out. He'd clear his throat. I'd kneel on my side of the divider, and I'd tell him about the girls that kept popping up in my mind, the candy I'd stolen from the station across the street from school, the lies I'd told my dad. And when I left, it was like a musty, wet blanket had been pulled off me, and the feeling would last a few days.

Standing there looking down at Father O'Neil's headstone, I wondered if I was still capable of that relief. I knelt down on his grave, gripping the cane with both hands until I'd gotten myself into position. Then I looked at the patch of grass he lay beneath and whispered: "I killed my wife."

But I didn't feel any different. I got to my feet as quickly as I could and went to Kimmy's.

About the Author

Dominic Stabile lives in Charleston, South Carolina. His short fiction has appeared in *The Horror Zine, Hellfire Crossroads Vol.3, Atticus Review*, and numerous other magazines. This is his first of many books to come. Visit his website at dominicstabile.com and like him on Facebook.

About the Author

www.ingramcontent.com/pod-product-compliance
Lightning Source LLC
Chambersburg PA
CBHW020140180626
46810CB00004B/1661